PRAISE FOR

NANCY J. CAVANAUGH

★ "A book that is full of surprises... Triumphant enough to make readers cheer; touching enough to make them cry."

—*Kirkus Reviews*, Starred Review on
This Journal Belongs to Ratchet

"Gators, huckleberry pie, and sweet tea on the porch are all part of the swamper way of life. Elsie Mae is spunky, headstrong, and kind... Swamp magic."

—*Kirkus Reviews* on *Elsie Mae Has Something to Say*

"Cavanaugh's sweet and engaging historical fiction style perfectly captures the special quality of life in the Okefenokee, from 'gators to biscuits to good neighbors. Elsie Mae is a strong, complicated heroine, surrounded by complex characters."

—*School Library Journal* on
Elsie Mae Has Something to Say

"From pillow fights to pinkie promises, sock wars to s'mores, a red thread connects this energetic summer camp story with Julia's deeper journey to accept herself, her adoption, and her Chinese roots."

—Megan McDonald, award-winning and bestselling author of the Judy Moody series and Sisters Club trilogy on *Just Like Me*

"[A] charming and refreshingly wholesome coming-of-age story... Filled with slapstick humor and fast-paced action."

—*School Library Journal* on *Just Like Me*

"Told in the hyper-chatty, status-obsessed voice of your secretly sweet best friend, *Always, Abigail* is always adorable."

—Tim Federle, author of *Better Nate Than Ever* on *Always, Abigail*

"Brimming with honesty and heart."

—Caroline Starr Rose, award-winning author of *May B.* on *Always, Abigail*

"Perfect for anyone who feels she doesn't belong."

—*Discovery Girls* magazine on *This Journal Belongs to Ratchet*

ALSO BY NANCY J. CAVANAUGH

This Journal Belongs to Ratchet

Always, Abigail

Just Like Me

Elsie Mae Has Something to Say

WHEN I HIT THE ROAD

WHEN I HIT the ROAD

NANCY J. CAVANAUGH

 sourcebooks
young readers

Copyright © 2020 by Nancy J. Cavanaugh
Cover and internal design © 2020 by Sourcebooks
Cover design and illustration © Risa Rodil
Internal design by Danielle McNaughton/Sourcebooks
Internal illustrations © 9george/Shutterstock
Internal illustrations by Travis Hasenour/Sourcebooks

Sourcebooks and the colophon are registered trademarks of Sourcebooks.

Published by Sourcebooks Young Readers, an imprint of Sourcebooks Kids
P.O. Box 4410, Naperville, Illinois 60567-4410
(630) 961-3900
sourcebookskids.com

Library of Congress Cataloging-in-Publication data is on file with the publisher.

This product conforms to all applicable CPSC and CPSIA standards.

Source of Production: Maple Press, York, Pennsylvania, United States
Date of Production: March 2020
Run Number: 5017722

Printed and bound in the United States of America.
MA 10 9 8 7 6 5 4 3 2 1

In loving memory of you, Susan, because none of my memories

or stories would be the same if I hadn't had you

for a sister, because I wouldn't be the same.

And in loving memory of my grandparents, Lenora & Harry

and Marguerite & Everett: There's nothing like the love that comes

from grandparents and the memories that grow out of that love.

I'm blessed to have had you for grandmas and grandpas.

DEAR ME,

As soon as Mom came up with Operation Sunny Sandy Shores, I knew I had no choice but to write these Dear Me letters.

Who else besides the future me would want to know every little detail of what I'm about to go through?

Of course, you already know how it all turns out. But I don't. Which is why I told Mom I'm filled with a slight feeling of dread.

(Mom, of course, says I'm being overly dramatic, but you and I both know that's not true.)

I don't have to tell you that once Mom gets something into her head, there's no stopping her. I bet a million trillion dollars she's still like that. Who knows? Maybe she's even worse.

But you're lucky. You're probably old enough by now that she can't boss you around anymore. I'm still in her sphere of supreme rule, which means when she says she's taking me with her to spend two weeks visiting Gram at her new condo at Sunny Sandy Shores Condominium Complex in Florida, there's nothing left to do but start packing.

Any of this sound familiar yet?

I sure hope so, because if not, that might mean this trip turned out <u>so</u> badly, you blocked the whole thing out of your mind, so you'd never have to think about it again.

Too bad <u>you</u> can't write <u>me</u> a letter. Then I'd at least have a hint of what's about to happen to me.

LOVE,
ME

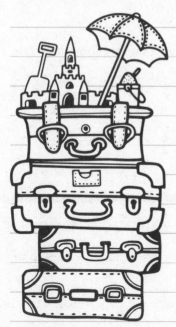

OPERATION: SUNNY SANDY SHORES

DEAR ME,

Maybe you're thinking, "Wow, I must've been a really brilliant twelve-year-old to think of writing letters to my future self."

But, if you're thinking that, you must've forgotten that Mom's the real reason I'm writing these letters.

Remember Make It, Take It, Live It, Give It? The crafts, gifts, and photo album company where Mom works? Well, the Dear Me Journal is her most recent brainstorm.

Dear Me Journals

RECORD IT TODAY, CHERISH IT TOMORROW.

Dear Me Journals are a revolutionary way of journaling.
Don't just write "Dear diary."
Don't just keep a log of your life.
Make it even more memorable.
Make it even more personal.
Write "Dear Me" letters to your future self.
Dear Me Journals—a way to do something unforgettable for the future you.

Dear Me Journal prototypes overflow from every tote bag Mom owns. So, since she'd forgotten to pick up a new spiral notebook for me to use for my summer journal, she tossed one of her Dear Me Journals onto my bed. Each journal comes with a cutesy carrying case, a pocketful of envelopes, and thematic decorative stickers. (Ugh! I mean, c'mon Mom, I'm going to be in seventh grade next year. Stickers? Really?)

But even though I gave Mom the are-you-kidding-me look when that Dear Me Journal practically landed in my lap, she didn't even acknowledge my annoyance. Her mind was way too focused on Operation Sunny Sandy Shores as well as her big Dear Me Journal presentation coming up next month at Make It, Take It.

Before I even had time to pick up the Dear Me Journal, Mom came running back into my room and exploded with enthusiasm, "I just had the most amazing idea, Samantha!"

But here's the thing, I knew from experience, which means you know it too, that if I had even one dollar for every time Mom said she had an <u>amazing</u> idea—even though the ideas weren't amazing <u>at all</u>—I'd be writing this letter from the deck of the cruise ship I was able to buy with all that money.

Mom's voice got even more ecstatic. "If you write Dear Me letters to yourself while we're in Florida, recording all your memorable moments with Gram, I'll include the letters in my Dear Me proposal presentation next month!"

I gave Mom the you-have-to-be-out-of-your-mind look.

But she continued anyway, telling me it would be an authentic example of just how fun and versatile these Dear Me Journals could be.

To that I said, "What?! No way! I'm not letting a bunch of strangers read what I write. I'm using it for a <u>journal</u>, Mom! A journal is <u>private</u>. As in, <u>personal</u>. As in, <u>not</u> public. Forget it!"

But you know how full of optimistic enthusiasm Mom is. My objections didn't even dampen her exuberance <u>one little bit</u>.

She told me to use the Dear Me Journal she'd already given me for my personal journal, and she'd give me another one to write letters in.

"It's a win-win situation, Sam," she said, sounding super excited.

Are you thinking what I'm thinking?

Win-win?

For <u>who</u>?

But I kept my mouth shut. I hoped my silence was enough to let Mom know her little plan was <u>not</u> going to happen.

But we both know Mom. Later, when I was in the shower, she put another Dear Me Journal on my bed with a lightbulb-shaped sticky note stuck to it that read, "Just think about it!"

So, that's how I ended up writing Dear Me letters.

But I'm not doing it for Mom.

Or the executives at Make It, Take It.

I'm doing it for me.

And for you.

So, <u>you're</u> the only one who's going to get to read them.

I don't plan on letting Mom even know I'm writing them.

TOP SECRET!

LOVE,
ME

DEAR ME,

Florida

Tallahassee
Jacksonville
Orlando
Tampa
Miami

So, according to Mom's product description, these letters are supposed to be chock-full of cherish-worthy memories. But don't get your hopes up, because here's the thing... Mom's pretending this is a friendly visit to spend time with Gram at her new condo and that it will be nothing but a memory-making fun-fest for the three of us. But Operation Sunny Sandy Shores, or OSSS (that's what I'm going to start calling it because I can't keep writing out that long name every single time) is all about Mom making her case that Gram should've never even moved to Florida.

Mom had the perfect little condo—which was exactly eight and a half minutes from our house without traffic—all picked out for Gram after Grandpa died. But Gram said she'd always wanted to live in Florida and had never had the chance, so that was what she was going to do.

Does this seem like a problem to you?

No. Of course not.

But it was a huuuuuge problem for Mom, "who always

knows best." But, because no one in our family really "fights" or "argues" out in the open, when Mom talked to Gram on the phone, she just kept saying things to Gram like, "Well, if that's what you really want..."

And then she'd sigh.

It was classic, I'll-be-polite-on-the-outside-even-though-I'm-not-happy-about-this-situation-on-the-inside Mom behavior.

(Mom should probably win an Oscar or something for how convincing she can be, except to people like you and me who can see right through her little act.)

Anyway, once Gram moved to Florida, Mom began laying the groundwork for her new plan.

After every phone call with her, Mom would say (to no one in particular) things like, "Something just doesn't seem right with her..." Or, "I'm really becoming concerned about her well-being."

You and I both know this is code for one thing. Mom was devising one of her I'll-take-control-of-this-situation-one-way-or-another strategies.

So, she put her let's-get-Gram-a-condo-near-us plan on the back burner and set OSSS into motion. It was a two-step rescue-and-recovery mission, with a very simple, straightforward objective:

1. Find just enough things in Gram's new life in disarray to make a case that moving to Florida was a big mistake.

2. Bring Gram back to Illinois and get her that condo eight and a half minutes from our house before it goes off the market.

I know Mom really believes Gram needs rescuing. But what does she think? That she's the Coast Guard? The National Guard? The I'm-gonna-save-my-mom-from-enjoying-a-new-life-in-Florida Guard? I mean, c'mon, Mom. Gram obviously doesn't think she needs rescuing, so I say let her be.

The problem is that no matter how Gram is really doing when we get there, Mom's going to "creatively" interpret the situation so that OSSS is a success. You and I both know this is just a nice way to say that Mom will make stuff up to fit her plan. And now, since I'm going with her, I feel like I'm an accomplice.

Besides not liking that I'm Mom's little minion on this mission, I'm only slightly excited to visit Gram. And if you're thinking that sounds terrible, then you must not remember the reason for my marginal amount of enthusiasm.

Gram and Grandpa lived pretty far from us, so we didn't

see them all that often. Since Mom and Dad were always tied up with work—and Tori, Annalise, and I were always busy with school and other stuff—there never seemed to be time for our family to make the eight-hour drive to visit them.

And that long drive was the same reason they rarely came to visit us, especially once Grandpa was diagnosed with his heart condition.

The few times I <u>do</u> remember visiting them, it wasn't all that fun. It's not that I didn't like Gram and Grandpa. It was just that their fancy furniture, white carpeting, and breakables on every end table meant a lot "sitting still" and "being good." I don't think any kid would think that was fantastically fun.

So, we really weren't all that close.

But that wasn't the only thing dampening my eagerness. I had a sneaking suspicion that this Sunny Sandy Shores

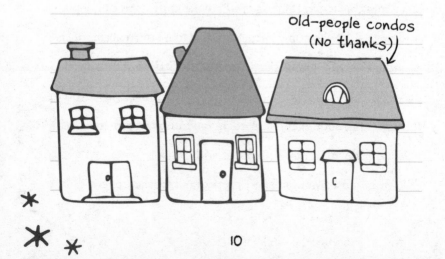

Old-people condos
(No thanks))

Condominium Complex where Gram had moved was one of those senior citizen communities I'd seen advertised on TV that showed all kinds of old people playing cards and wandering on walking paths, smiling and laughing with each other.

So, I've kind of been being a brat about the trip, whining and complaining. All the while, Mom continues spreading her positive, optimistic attitude all over the place.

"Most people would love to be going to Florida for a couple weeks," she says smiling.

"Not if you're going to an old people's home," I say back.

To spy on your grandma, I want to say, but don't.

"I bet you'll end up having the time of your life!" Mom continues in that overexaggerated cheerful voice.

You know the voice I'm talking about, right? That always-see-the-glass-half-full voice.

Then I say, "If spending time at an old people's home is the time of my life, I should just crawl under the nearest rock, curl up, and die right now to save myself the misery."

I know this is a little dramatic, even for me, so I'm not surprised when Mom uses her I'm-at-the-end-of-my-rope voice to say, "Samantha, stop being so dramatic!"

Then she adds matter-of-factly, with very little cheerfulness left in her voice, "And I've told you a <u>million</u> times, Sunny Sandy Shores is <u>not</u> an old people's home. It's just a regular condominium complex."

"What do you wanna bet all the people are gonna be old?" I say, pushing my luck, knowing full well that I've likely just gotten on Mom's last nerve.

Then she glares at me with that you're-tipping-over-my-half-full-glass look. And I know to put a lid on it before that glass of hers tips all the way over and breaks.

You're all grown up now, but does she still give you that look sometimes?

I sure hope, by the time you read this letter, you're old enough to give Mom that same look right back without getting into trouble.

LOVE,
ME

DEAR ME,

Do you remember much about sixth grade?

Well, just in case your memory is failing a little, I think it's important to remind you of a few details.

My goal when I got to middle school was to be able to tape a practice or rehearsal schedule up on the fridge next to Tori's varsity volleyball schedule and Annalise's concert piano schedule. So, I set out to find my "thing."

But here are the top ten reasons why that never happened:

1. I hit seven balls over the fence during tennis tryouts and didn't get one single serve inbounds.
2. I fell doing a cartwheel and twisted my ankle at dance squad auditions.
3. In volleyball tryouts, I never got a single ball over the net but managed to get one spiked in my face.
4. I pulled a muscle trying to kick as high as everyone else at cheerleading tryouts, and Mom had to take me to physical therapy for a month.
5. I tripped on the ball running down the

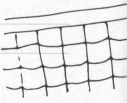

field at soccer tryouts and literally ended up with grass stains on my chin.

6. Trying to qualify for the math decathlon, I didn't even make it past the first placement test.

7. I hit two people in the head with a giant prop candy cane and knocked over the Styrofoam streetlamp at the holiday showcase auditions.

8. The school nurse had to be called when I landed on the high-jump bar during indoor track tryouts. (I was pretty sure I broke my back, so Mom took me to the urgent care center, but it ended up only being a bad bone bruise.)

9. I whiffed the ball six times at bat during softball tryouts and face-planted trying to catch a grounder.

10. The details of the Spring Fine Arts Festival auditions are so horrific that I would be super surprised if you don't remember it like it was yesterday. Even so, I promise to write more about it later, but it will require me to devote an entire letter to that subject alone.

Maybe you're wondering why I was such a glutton for

punishment, but here's the thing: all these disastrous tryouts surprised me. In elementary school, I had joined lots of teams/groups/clubs. So, I just assumed middle school would be the same. But here's the other thing: in elementary school, everyone makes the team or gets into the group or can be part of 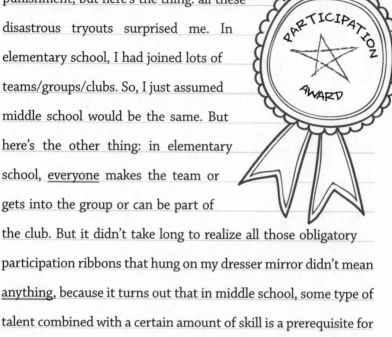 the club. But it didn't take long to realize all those obligatory participation ribbons that hung on my dresser mirror didn't mean anything, because it turns out that in middle school, some type of talent combined with a certain amount of skill is a prerequisite for everything you do. And from the list above, it's extremely obvious that I was lacking both in all the things that really mattered.

It seems impossible, with sisters like Tori and Annalise, that there isn't something I'm exceptionally good at. But with each new epic fail, it became harder and harder for me to believe that I possessed an adeptness for anything at all. Even so, I kept signing up to try out for things because of Mom's mantra of "Keep trying!" or "Your perseverance will pay off eventually!"

This did not turn out to be good advice for someone like me, and sixth grade became a long, arduous year.

I planned to spend my summer searching for that overlooked aptitude that just <u>had</u> to be inside me somewhere. That way, I'd have time to master and perfect it before the start of seventh grade. But now, just because I'm not off at sports camp like Tori or participating in the downtown music conservatory like Annalise this summer, Mom has recruited me for her OSSS mission. So, I don't see how I'll have time to discover any hidden talents that might be lurking below the surface somewhere deep inside me.

LOVE,
ME

DEAR ME,

I really wish you had been there to see Mom's face when we spotted Gram in the baggage-claim area when we landed in Florida.

(Oh, that's right, <u>technically</u> you were there.)

Anyway, Gram was easy to spot, that was for sure—a baggy, bright, orange-juice-colored T-shirt with the words, "Sunshine Sisters" printed on it and sparkly silver and gold flip-flops with foofy, plastic flowers on them.

This was not at all the way Gram looked when she used to greet us in the doorway of her old house as she made sure we took off our shoes <u>outside</u> the door so as not to dirty up her beloved white carpeting.

Gram told us we were "a sight for sore eyes," and enveloped Mom and me (at the same time) in a huge hug, squeezing us both so tight I felt like she was trying to deflate us. When she finally let go, Mom and I both told Gram how glad we were to see her.

(Her hug really <u>did</u> make me glad to see her.)

"So, 'Sunshine Sisters,' Mother? Who are they?" Mom said stepping back from Gram and looking at her shirt.

Mom asked the question so casually that anyone who didn't know her would never realize there were many more questions hammering around in her head, like "Why aren't you wearing a sensible pair of sandals instead of those gaudy flip-flops?" or "What made you think it was a good idea to go out in public dressed in a sloppy T-shirt instead of something more prudent, like a nice polo or pullover?"

And even though those questions on the surface sound kind of snarky, in Mom's defense, which are three words you might be surprised to hear me say, Mom really can't help asking questions like that in situations like this. Mom thinks presentation is everything. It's just how she is. So, seeing Gram dressed in such an ill-mannered way probably raised all the hairs on the back of her neck and made her feel like she was possibly going to break out in hives.

Gram held my hand as the three of us walked toward the luggage carousal, and she explained, with a grin that was bigger than the hug she'd given us, that the "Sunshine Sisters" was the nickname the pickleball group had given her and her partner.

Gram went on to tell us that pickleball was a ball-and-paddle sport (which I already knew from gym class), but what I didn't know was that my grandma was now playing this sport with enough frequency to actually have a partner.

The look on Mom's face told me that her next question wasn't going to be about flip-flops, polo shirts, or pullovers. And I was correct in my assumption, because what Mom said next was, "Pickleball?!"

To which Gram answered, "I know. Weird to think I'm playing any kind of sport, isn't it? But it's a real hoot!"

And all I could think was that the weirdness of Gram playing pickleball was one thing, but Gram uttering a sentence with the word "hoot" in it was way past weird. It was about as absurd as me being voted best all-around athlete or first-chair musician in my middle school. And even though, most of the time, I'm pretty sure I know exactly what Mom is thinking and what she's likely to say next, this moment was so out of the ordinary, I had no idea.

But if you think that's mind-boggling, wait until you hear what happened when we left the terminal.

Gram led us outside to the parking lot and stopped behind a red Mustang convertible.

"Mother, what are you doing?" Mom asked sounding like the effects of our early morning flight coupled with the unexpectedness we were experiencing with Gram so far was causing her to get a little irritated.

But when Gram clicked her key fob and the trunk of the Mustang opened, Mom's irritation morphed into what I would call slightly confused shock.

And both Mom and I said together, at exactly the same time, like it was a rehearsed line of dialogue from a play, "You're driving a Mustang convertible?!"

"Don't you just love it?" Gram asked giggling.

Well, I don't have to tell you that Mom didn't giggle.

Flip-flops and T-shirts were one thing, but a convertible Mustang that Mom didn't know about was in a whole different league.

But I didn't giggle either.

I laughed my head off.

This was awesome! I had a grandma who was driving a Mustang convertible!

"What happened to the Impala?" Mom asked.

"That old thing? I traded it in," Gram said. "I didn't mention it because you would've told me I was nuttier than a box of Cracker Jack buying a convertible at my age."

Mom wouldn't have said it like that, but whatever she did say, and whatever she was thinking at the moment, meant the exact same thing.

Gram finished by saying, "But I don't care, because I love it!"

Gram driving around in a Mustang with the top down hardly proved that she needed rescuing. If you ask me, it proved the exact opposite.

It also maybe proved something else that made me really glad. Maybe the Mustang proved that Gram wasn't quite as sad about Grandpa as she'd been the last time we'd seen her.

"A red convertible was actually the first thing on my WBL,"  Gram said as we got into the car.

"WBL?" I asked. "What's a WBL?"

"Yes, Mother," Mom said. "What, pray tell, is a WBL?"

"A widow's bucket list," Gram said matter-of-factly.

"A widow's bucket list?!" Mom and I said in unison again.

"You've heard of a bucket list—a list of things people want to do before they die."

"Yes, Mother, I know what a bucket list is."

"Well, since your father died, God rest his soul, my list is a widow's bucket list."

"Is there something besides the Mustang you're not telling me?" Mom asked.

"Just that the Mustang is only the beginning."

"What's <u>that</u> supposed to mean?" Mom said sounding concerned.

"You'll see," Gram said in a singsongy voice.

Mom took a deep breath and sighed loudly, but I laughed again as Gram turned and winked at me in the back seat.

Then Gram reached into the glove compartment and pulled out a leopard-print scarf.

What happened next is an example of the challenge involved in hanging out with old people. They do really wacky things, sometimes without even realizing how utterly inappropriate they are.

Gram folded the scarf in half diagonally, put it on her head, and tied it snugly under her chin.

(If you want to know the truth, she looked like a cleaning woman who had just stolen a sports car.)

Maybe you've forgotten by now that Gram was always paranoid about messing up her hair. I guess she wasn't going to take any chances that any of her straw-like strands of hairspray-coated hair would fly in the wind as we drove with the top down.

But the wackiness didn't stop with the scarf.

Next, she reached into her purse and pulled out a pair of sunglasses.

She told us she was lucky to get such a good deal on her new prescription driving sunglasses.

"They're just perfect for the Florida sunshine," she said sounding proud.

She took off her regular glasses and let them hang from a chain around her neck.

The prescription driving glasses she put on wrapped all the way around the side of her head. Now she looked like a picture from a chapter in my sixth-grade social studies book—"Women Welders Help the War Effort."

The amusement of watching Mom get exasperated with

Gram trickled away like the sweat that dripped down the back of my legs as I squirmed on the hot leather seats of Gram's Mustang. The "coolness" of riding around in a convertible was just not enough to erase the embarrassment of Gram driving that convertible while wearing a leopard-print babushka and welder-war-effort sunglasses.

You're probably wondering what in the world happens next. And believe me, as Gram ran over three curbs driving the Mustang out of the parking lot, I was wondering the exact same thing.

LOVE,
ME

DEAR ME,

So, because I don't know exactly how old you are or how much you remember about your past, there are a few things I think you need to know so that none of the angst of all that I'm going through gets lost.

Neither one of us wants that.

I don't know if you remember Mrs. Brackman, my sixth-grade language arts teacher, but she was this huge proponent of vocabulary cultivation/acquisition, as she called it.

(You probably guessed that *proponent* was one of our vocabulary words. You may also have noticed that I've already sprinkled quite a few of her words into my letters. Thanks for noticing!)

Anyway, Mrs. Brackman loved to say, "Remember, people, words not only allow us to communicate, but they also define us."

(You may still remember this quote word for word because she said it about five thousand times in nine months.)

We literally learned hundreds of vocabulary words throughout the year, and she quizzed us on them incessantly.

(And yes, you guessed it, "incessantly" is another vocab word. I promise not to incessantly point them out anymore. I'll just let you find them on your own.)

Well, I found that every time I slipped a vocab word into a conversation with Mom, she usually commented on how I was being overly dramatic again, which made me want to string together entire sentences of vocabulary words every single time I spoke to her. (Who knows? Maybe you still do that just to bug her.)

I'd say things like, "Due to Mrs. Brackman's propensity to relentlessly delve into the variety of ways words can be utilized, I have spent the school day being irked immensely and am therefore utterly exasperated and incapable of cleaning my room."

Man, did Mom ever hate when I said things like that!

It never got me out of any work around the house or impress upon Mom the agony of the personal academic plight I faced daily at school, but all that extra vocabulary practice made me a vocab expert. So, I only missed two words all year.

(I try not to use vocab words when I talk to classmates and friends, because even though everyone knows adults might be impressed with big, long, stuffy words, kids are definitely not.)

Anyway, the day after our final vocabulary quiz, Mrs. Brackman made a colossal deal out of my overall vocabulary score, which was extraordinarily better than anyone else's. She said she wished there was a special award she could give me for having the top vocabulary score, but then she said my reward was how well prepared I would be in life to, you guessed it, "communicate and define myself with words." And <u>that</u> after all, was much more valuable than any award she could give.

Doesn't that sound amazing?

You and I both know that the answer to that question is a monumental "NO!" There's nothing amazing about not being good at any of the things that really count and being exceptionally good at something that no one except a vocabulary virtuoso like Mrs. Brackman is ever going to notice.

So, you might kind of cringe when I remind you that I created in my mind the Sixth-Grade Vocabulary Victor Award. I wrote about it in my journal, but then, when I reread the journal entry a week later, I realized how much of an SAP-o-saurus I was for

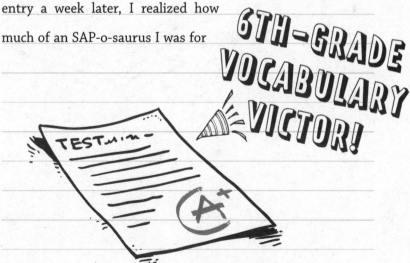

6TH-GRADE VOCABULARY VICTOR!

TEST

A+

making up an award for myself, and I ended up feeling worse than pathetic.

LOVE,

ME

P.S. Just so you know, **SAP-O-SAURUS** is an example of what Mrs. Brackman would call a "horrific slang term," which makes it nearly impossible, according to Mrs. Brackman, for people to communicate with one another with any degree of accuracy. But I think, when used correctly, as I have done here, that "SAP-o-saurus" allows me to communicate something for which there is no other word.

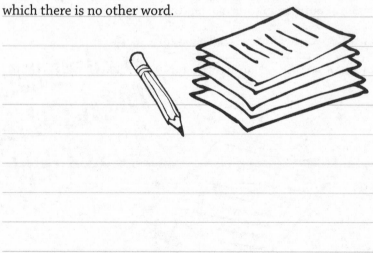

DEAR ME,

One thing I was actually looking forward to about going to Florida was lying at the condo pool chilling out.

That's what summer's for, right?

But my very first visit to the pool proved to be more than a little disturbing.

As soon as I chose a lounge chair and sat down, I noticed a lady sitting across the pool from me wearing some old-fashioned thing that I think was supposed to be a swimsuit, but honestly, I don't know what it was. If it was a swimsuit, I should've called the police, and I'm not talking about the fashion police, I'm talking about the real police, because she obviously had stolen this historic swimsuit from some museum's antiquated clothing exhibit. And the hat she wore was as big as a satellite dish. I bet she could've picked up at least a thousand TV channels with that thing.

Another lady in the pool wore a swim cap decorated with different-colored rubber flowers on top of it and with a chin strap to hold it on her head. She bobbed up and down and jumped around in the water. I think she thought she

was exercising, but she looked like a drowning ladybug. She flailed her arms and legs so wildly I was afraid if I got into the water, she might pull me to the bottom of the pool and drown me.

And as if that wasn't enough to dash my dreams of relaxing in the Florida sunshine, sitting down by the deep end was a guy who looked like he had to be a <u>least</u> a hundred years old. He wore huge headphones with an antenna sticking out of one side, and he sang opera songs at the top of his lungs in Italian.

The new earbuds I bought for the trip could never mute Opera Man's loud, off-key singing voice, so I left the pool before it was even time to put on more sunscreen.

Back upstairs, Mom sat at Gram's dining room table typing a mile a minute on her laptop with her Make It, Take It stuff strewn all over the place.

(So much for our trip to Florida being a magical time of mother-and-daughter memory-making and bonding.)

Before I go further with what happened next, I should tell you that, even though the condo pool had turned into a mega letdown so soon after arriving at Sunny Sandy Shores, the condition of Gram's condo was a mammoth relief. I was delighted that, when Mom and I walked in, we found that the condo did <u>not</u> resemble Gram's old house one bit.

Gram gave us a tour of her place while still wearing her silver and gold flip-flops, which was alarming, due to the fact that I had never seen her wear outside shoes inside the house ever before. While we walked from room to room, Gram bragged about the easy-to-keep-clean, multicolored beige carpeting that didn't show lint, dirt, or spills of any kind.

She told us she loved her new, cute, comfortable, white wicker furniture, which she'd gotten on clearance at the Why Not Wicker store her new condo friends had told her about. And then she pointed out the expertly placed seashells on the end tables and coffee table, which she told us were "welcome gifts" from all the people who lived on the floor of her condo building, and "Wasn't that a nice way to be welcomed to Sunny Sandy Shores?"

Near each one of the "welcome" seashells, there was a different framed family photo, and, from what we could see, those photos were the only things left from Gram's old house.

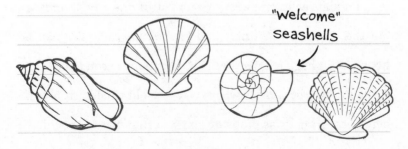

"Welcome" seashells

Mom wanted to know what happened to all of Gram's stuff.

"I wanted a fresh start... So, once the house sold, a friend of mine told me about Junk to Gems Estate Sales. They came in and took care of everything for me."

"Why in the world would you do that?" Mom asked.

"Why wouldn't I?" Gram said. "I asked you if you wanted anything from the house, and you didn't..."

"Yes, but I didn't know you were getting rid of it all," Mom said.

"Well, it was my decision, and I decided to take the memories and sell the stuff," Gram said sounding proud of herself. "Besides, it was nice to have some extra money to buy new things for the condo."

Mom's frustrated sigh said it all, but there was really no logical argument against what Gram had decided to do, especially from Mom.

After all, her career was based on helping people preserve memories, and it sounded like Gram had the right idea.

I didn't really care about Gram's stuff one way or another, but the revelation that her condo wasn't anything like her old house was a huge relief, especially now that the condo pool had turned out to be a place where way-out old-timers sat around being eccentric. I was probably going to find myself spending a

lot more time <u>inside</u> Gram's condo. I was grateful that I wouldn't have to tiptoe around on white carpeting in socks or worry about the possibility of coughing or sneezing too hard and smashing to smithereens some expensive chunk of china.

When I sat down at the dining room table across from Mom to tell her about all the horrors I'd seen on my first trip to the Sunny Sandy Shores pool, I whispered because I didn't want Gram to hear me describing her eccentric neighbors, who, for all I knew, were part of the seashell-delivering welcome wagon Gram was so fond of.

Mom stopped typing, ignored my detailed pool report, and told me that Gram had gone somewhere while I was gone.

"She was all secretive about where she was going and said it was all part of some <u>big</u> surprise," Mom added sounding sort of miffed.

Then Mom's phone rang, and you probably guessed it. It was work.

And the second Mom said "Hello," her voice changed from a slightly annoyed tone to an enthusiastic, optimistic, cheerful one.

At the same time, there was a knock at the door. Mom motioned for me to go answer it, and when I did, I found a little old lady standing in the hallway outside Gram's door.

She smiled at me and said, "Look at you, honey!"

This lady had such skinny arms and legs sticking out of her brightly colored, floral dress that she looked more like a marionette who had fallen into a flower bed than an actual person.

The flower-bed-puppet lady reached out and squeezed my arm with her skinny, twig-like fingers and said, "You're even more precious than your grandmother said you were."

Now maybe by the time you're reading this letter you're so old that it doesn't seem strange that someone would describe a middle schooler as "precious" but I've got to tell you that it's just...not normal.

"After I knocked, I realized your grandmother wouldn't be home yet from her voice lesson. I can hardly believe it's her last one before the first big contest."

The words "voice lesson" and "contest" when talking about Gram caused the wheels of my mind to screech to a halt like someone slamming on the brakes to avoid a crash.

"I'm Mildred, by the way, but you can call me Mimi," the marionette said as she squeezed my arm again with her twig fingers.

Her gigantic grin kept getting more and more gigantic.

But even with her massive, gigantic, friendly grin, I was

pretty sure I would not be calling this lady Mildred or Mimi because I wasn't planning on the two of us getting all that close.

Mildred/Mimi called me "honey" again and asked if I'd let Gram know that she was leaving the Bibles so that we could load them in the car in the morning while we waited for her to finish with her prayer meeting.

That's when I noticed a stack of boxes, almost as tall as Mimi, sitting on a dolly next to Gram's door.

Then she said, "Thank heavens for Harold" helping her get the boxes of Bibles down to the third floor, and that she sure couldn't have done it herself. She wished Harold had been able to stick around so I could meet him, because she was sure I would love him.

Since I didn't know this Harold person Mildred was talking about, I didn't necessarily have any reason to think I wouldn't like him, but I wondered what made Mildred think I would undoubtedly adore him.

Then, for some reason, Mimi felt compelled to tell me that Harold had rushed off to his appointment at the foot doctor, because he had some toe fungus, and she was just thankful that he was finally getting it checked out even though he hated doctors.

"I told him that the yellow and green pus wasn't going to go away on its own," Mildred finished with a sigh.

Are you thinking what I'm thinking?

Toe fungus?

Yellow and green pus?

Too much information!

And, ICK!

"Oh, just listen to me going on and on," Mildred said and squeezed my arm for the third time. "I'm just so tickled we're all going on this trip together. It's going to be such a hoot!"

Well, that explained where Gram had learned her new vocabulary word, but it did not explain anything about something that was much more important.

Trip?

What trip?

I wish I knew the antonym for "hoot," because that would be the only way to describe what it's going to be like when Gram explains to Mom and me what in the world Mildred was talking about.

LOVE,
ME

DEAR ME,

So, of all the things I've written so far, what I'm about to tell you has got to be the wildest.

Gram's big surprise for Mom and me?

Are you ready for this?

Drum roll, please...

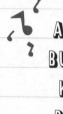

A WIDOW'S BUCKET LIST KARAOKE ROAD TRIP

And Mom and I are going with her.

I know. Pretty bonkers, right?

And you probably already guessed that Mimi and her boxes of Bibles are going along too.

(Apparently, she's planning to deliver the Bibles to some churches for their Vacation Bible School programs.)

"You're standing there in front of me saying 'widow's bucket list karaoke road trip' as if it's the most normal thing in the world."

That's what Mom said when Gram came back from her voice lesson and told us all about the big surprise.

"Well, it *is* normal if you're a widow and you've always wanted to sing karaoke."

That's what Gram said.

"Don't you think it's just a little outside the norm, Mother, for someone at your age to be driving all over the state of Florida singing karaoke?"

Though at this point, the family's politeness-no-matter-what rule remained in place, with each thing Mom said, I wondered when it was going to start leaning like the Tower of Pisa. Under the circumstances, I did not see how things were not going to lean so far, they'd eventually come crashing down.

But here's the thing. Before Mom and I had gotten to Florida and been greeted by Gram's new-surprise-every-second behavior, I would've agreed with Mom's opinion that a person as old as Gram singing karaoke was outside the norm. Actually, Gram doing any of the stuff we'd witnessed since we arrived was way outside the norm. But it was obvious that when Gram moved to Florida, she hadn't just changed her address.

She wasn't just wearing new clothes and new shoes and driving a new car.

She wasn't just suddenly playing a game called pickleball.

Her widow's bucket list karaoke road trip proved she might have actually <u>become</u> someone new. Someone I never knew she was. And from the way Mom was reacting, someone Mom had never known she was either.

I sort of thought all of it was pretty...cool. But Mom thought all of it was extremely ridiculous.

"And how in the world did this Bible lady get involved in this road trip?" Mom asked, using air quotes for "Bible lady" and letting her voice creep toward the immensely irked level.

Her use of air quotes and a sarcastic nickname for a little old lady proved her evolving exasperation.

"Oh, Mildred?" Gram asked, as if there might be more than one person at Sunny Sandy Shores who could fit the description of "Bible lady."

"Mildred's the other Sunshine Sister. My pickleball partner."

At this point, I laughed. Out loud.

I shouldn't have.

It was rude.

I didn't like when people laughed at me.

But the <u>only</u> thing more impossible than picturing Gram singing karaoke or playing a game called pickleball was picturing

the tiny, spindly, marionette lady named Mildred playing pickle-ball with Gram.

But Gram didn't even get mad at me or scold me for laughing.

She just chuckled and said, "I'm sure it's a real hoot imagining the two of us out there on the courts, but we just have the best darn time."

Gram must've realized Mom was not finding any hilarity in all of this, because she just kept talking and went on to explain that she couldn't very well go on the road trip alone, and she didn't know for sure that Mom and I were coming until a couple weeks ago, so she and Mildred got to talking one Sunday after church, and they came up with the plan.

Gram told us that she'd spent the last few months taking voice lessons to prepare for the Seniors Got Talent karaoke contest put on by the Association of Florida Community Centers taking place all over south Florida. She'd have three chances to qualify for the big final competition taking place at the Florida's Fun in the Sun County Fair in Borlandsville.

She also told us that Mildred had spent the last few months collecting money to buy Bibles to donate to south Florida's churches in need.

"So, the two of us thought, why not put our ideas together?"

Then she added, "Mimi actually thinks it's a divinely inspired plan, and I have to agree."

I'll give you ten guesses who <u>didn't</u> agree, even though you'll only need one guess.

Mom was just about to say something when her phone rang again.

This time it was Dad. He had been overseas on a work trip when Mom and I left, so I knew Mom wouldn't want to miss his call.

But, since she was trying to come up with something else to say about everything Gram had just told us, she told me to go in the bedroom and talk to Dad. I was supposed to tell him she'd be there in a few minutes.

I was glad to have the chance to talk to Dad, especially since he hadn't been home when Mom and I left, but I was sorry to miss the continuation of the conflict/rumblings of a possible argument erupting between Mom and Gram.

You're probably dying to know what happens next. That's what I like about you. You think exactly like me.

LOVE,
ME

DEAR ME,

Are chocolate chip cookies still your favorite? If you don't like them anymore because you're sick of them, it's my fault. One of the things that got me through that long, arduous year of sixth grade was baking.

My specialty?

Chocolate chip cookies.

But, truthfully, you should really blame Mom more than me for the number of cookies I both baked and ate.

It started after tennis tryouts. When Mom picked me up, I didn't even have to tell her about those seven balls I hit over the fence into the softball field or about how many times I double-faulted when it was my turn to serve. She didn't even have to see my skinned elbow and scraped knee from when I skidded across the court going for an out-of-bounds ball. She could tell by the way I slammed the car door that tennis was definitely not going to be my "thing."

But you know as well as I do that Mom always has to be

True Love

43

eternally cheerful, so after she gave me her most current version of the you've-got-to-keep-trying speech, she told me to go home and bake something.

"It'll be good therapy!" she said sounding as if she was proud of herself for having such a good idea.

Well, even though I don't like to admit it, because that would mean Mom was right, baking really <u>was</u> good therapy. And that was fortunate for me, because, as you can tell from my earlier letters, as the school year dragged on, I needed <u>a lot</u> of therapy.

Anyway, baking in our kitchen was easy, because at one time Mom had worked in the creative cooking and baking division of Make It, Take It, so our cupboards were full of cookbooks, gadgets, and the best bakeware money could buy.

At first, I tried a few out-of-the-ordinary cupcake and cookie recipes, but soon chocolate chip cookies became my favorite thing to make. I made them so often that I not only memorized Mom's recipe, but by the end of the school year, I had also figured out a way to vary the ingredients to come up with a chocolate chip cookie that was even better than Mom's.

So, it didn't surprise me when I gave Gram a cookie from the tin I'd brought from home, after her first bite she said, "Samantha, these are the best darn cookies I think I've ever tasted!"

We were in the kitchen waiting for Mom to get off the phone from her <u>fifth</u> Make It, Take It phone call.

I knew Gram would compliment me on my cookies no matter what. After all, she was my grandma. But I could tell by the way she closed her eyes while she chewed and made a lot of "Mmmmm" sounds that she really did think they were extraordinarily good.

Gram wanted to know what in the world I did to make them taste so good.

But I never got the chance to tell her, because the kitchen door swung open, and Mom appeared.

"What are these?!" she asked, holding up two pill bottles.

Gram's jaw stopped midchew.

But Mom answered her own question.

"I know for a <u>fact</u> they're blood pressure and cholesterol medication!"

Gram didn't say anything.

I wasn't sure if she didn't answer Mom because she was scared or because Mom hadn't really given her a chance.

"You told me there were <u>no</u> issues at your last physical! What reason would you have for keeping something like this from me?"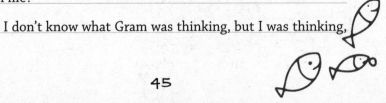

I don't know what Gram was thinking, but I was thinking,

"Well, Mom, the same reason Tori, Annalise, and I moved the bookshelf in the basement to cover the fruit punch we spilled on the new Berber carpeting.

"And the same reason we hid your good tablecloth after we used it by mistake for a drop cloth when we made tie-dyed T-shirts in the garage.

"Because you freak out too much, Mom!"

When I wrote in the last letter that the widow's bucket list karaoke Bible-delivery road trip was the craziest thing ever, that was because I didn't know how much crazier things were going to get.

I had seen Mom upset, angry, exasperated, infuriated, and on and on and on. I mean you should've heard her yell the day she moved that bookshelf while cleaning the basement and saw that fruit punch stain on the carpeting. And when Dad showed her the tablecloth after he found it hidden in the garage behind his tool bench... She pretty much went ballistic.

But even I was running out of vocab words to describe how all Gram's unexpected surprises seemed to be chipping away, little by little, at Mom's moxie. And now that Mom had found something that really was worthy of worry, I wondered if Gram would get into more trouble than Tori, Annalise, and I had because of the fruit punch spill and the tie-dye-splattered tablecloth.

But even as Mom flipped out, Gram stayed calm.

"There's nothing wrong with me except old age," she said. "I have high blood pressure and high cholesterol. So what? Who doesn't?"

"This is not a joke, Mother." Mom said. "We're talking about your health."

Through the controlled calm Mom mustered up on the outside, I could hear the strained annoyance coming through in her voice when she asked, "Is this what's behind this whole widow's bucket list nonsense?"

Gram didn't say anything to that, so Mom kept going and told Gram that this was exactly the kind of reason why she didn't want Gram moving all the way down here where she couldn't keep an eye on her.

Once Mom stopped talking, Gram stood up and stared her right in the face.

"You listen to me, sister! I might be old, and you might not

47

think I can handle things now that your dad is gone, but I'm still your mother. And I don't need your permission to do anything."

Can you believe Gram said that?!

But it gets even better—listen to this.

Gram took a deep breath, and then moved even closer to Mom and pointed her finger at her, "You just wait until you're seventy-seven. You'll know then that you don't have to be dying to realize you haven't had the chance to do everything you always wanted to do."

Then Gram pushed open the kitchen door and walked out, taking her chocolate chip cookie with her. But through the swinging door we heard her say, "And, by the way, my health is fine."

I don't know who was more surprised by Gram's stern scolding and finger wagging—Mom or me.

But it didn't matter.

It proved that this brand-new Gram, one we'd never seen before, was downright determined. It was obvious that Gram was not going to let anyone or anything stand in the way of who she now was and what she now planned to do.

LOVE,
ME

DEAR ME,

You would think that because it took Gram a couple hours to come out of her bedroom, Mom would've realized that she should be more agreeable. But sometimes Mom just can't give in.

When Gram came into the living room and asked us if we wanted to go out for burgers at Chattaway, Mom actually asked, "Do you really think burgers are a good idea with your high cholesterol?"

Was Mom clueless enough to actually think continuing the cholesterol conversation was the right choice?

But Gram wasn't going to be intimidated.

"Lynette, you've made it perfectly clear that you didn't want me to move to Florida. But I thought when you and Sam made plans to come down here, that you'd finally decided to respect my decision. But if that's not the case..."

She didn't finish what she was going to say, and I wondered if she was going to tell Mom that she better shape up or she would send both of us home.

For a few seconds no one talked. Gram and Mom just looked at each other like they were having a staring contest, and I waited to see who would look away first.

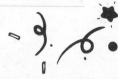

49

Thankfully, Mom backed down and had the good sense to quit questioning Gram about the wisdom of eating cholesterol-laden hamburgers. She called a truce by telling Gram she was "allowed to worry."

"You can worry all you want, but you're not allowed to tell me what to do, especially when it comes to things more important than you can imagine."

Ouch?!

Chalk one up for Gram, big-time.

"Now let's go get some juicy red meat, shall we?" Gram said. "I'm famished!"

So, about thirty minutes later, the three of us sat in Gram's convertible at the Chattaway drive-in restaurant, licking ketchup and mayonnaise and mustard off our fingers as we took huge bites of Chattaway's famous classic cheeseburgers, while washing it all down with Chattaway chocolate shakes.

The restaurant was shaped like a hamburger, and oldies music played from skinny speakers shaped

like french fries. I felt like we were in the middle of an old movie set, and even though Gram wore her three-cornered babushka scarf and her welder sunglasses and she had high blood pressure and high cholesterol and Mom's internal control freak was undoubtedly still freaking out somewhere below the surface and my first visit to the condo pool had turned out worse than I ever could've imagined, it didn't matter because each juicy bite of my burger and each satisfying slurp of my cool, creamy chocolate shake was quite possibly the best thing I'd ever tasted.

Halfway through her burger, with her mouth full of meat, Gram said, "Isn't this place just the cat's meow?"

Mom and I laughed, not only because of what Gram said, but also because Gram had mustard on her cheek and a massive mayonnaise stain on her bright orange T-shirt.

"We're a mess!" Mom said swiping her chin with a napkin just before burger juice dripped into her lap.

"I told you they were the best, didn't I?" Gram said laughing.

Mom agreed that it did hit the spot.

I raised up my shake cup, leaned in between the two front seats, and the three of us toasted.

It felt like a new beginning for us.

But I'm not getting too excited.

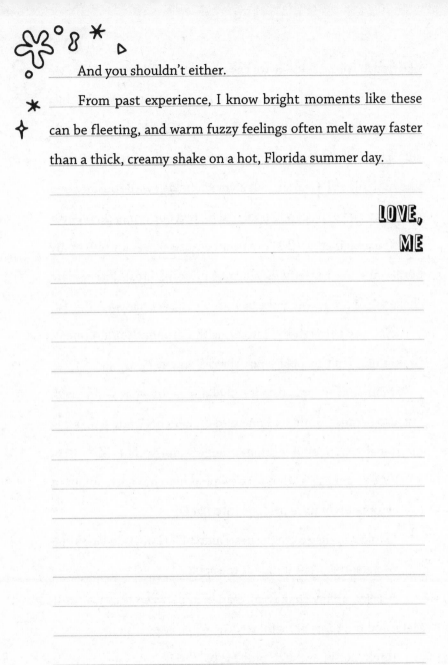

And you shouldn't either.

From past experience, I know bright moments like these can be fleeting, and warm fuzzy feelings often melt away faster than a thick, creamy shake on a hot, Florida summer day.

LOVE,
ME

DEAR ME,

I promised I'd fill you in on the details of the Spring Fine Arts Festival audition, so I guess now that you're in a good mood from the last letter about those mouthwatering burgers and those cool, creamy shakes at Chattaway, it's as good a time as any.

By April, I had made a pact with myself that I wouldn't try out or audition for anything else. To be truthful, there wasn't much left to try out for. But, in one last, desperate effort to make a name for myself in middle school, about a week after spring break, against my better judgment, I signed up to audition to sing a solo in the Sixth-Grade Spring Fine Arts Festival.

I dressed up in an old, raggedy, thrift-store dress, pretended to be Miss Hannigan from the musical *Annie*, and sang "Easy Street" for my audition.

But there was <u>nothing</u> easy about it.

It's not <u>easy</u> to make it to the end of a performance when you realize in the first few seconds that you don't belong anywhere near a stage <u>or</u> a microphone.

It's not <u>easy</u> to watch Mr. Grimson, Mrs. Palen, and Ms. Banford sit at the long table in the middle of the gym staring at you, disbelief covering their faces.

It's not <u>easy</u> to know what to say afterward when your friends and family ask, "So how'd it go?" because the answer to that question would be, "Well, I accomplished my goal. I made a name for myself, but not one I want anyone to remember."

Before the audition, I practiced for weeks in the basement. I had my performance all planned out—my hand gestures, my expressions, my little dance moves. I thought I looked <u>so</u> good. It never occurred to me how bad I might <u>sound</u>. But at the audition, from the very first note, I knew I had made a HUGE mistake. And it turns out, I was right.

Now that I'm about to head out on this widow's bucket list karaoke road trip, I'm worried I might have the same exact feeling when Gram gets up onstage to sing. What if <u>her</u> first note is as bad as mine was?

Making a fool of myself is one thing but having to sit in the

audience watching <u>Gram</u> possibly make a fool of herself is cringey enough to make me feel more nauseous than the time I ate sixteen of my just-out-of-the-oven chocolate chip cookies. The thought of it is really enough to make a person want to hurl.

LOVE,

ME

P.S. I remember thinking when I finished my audition that, as long as I lived, even if by some stroke of luck, I happened to live longer than anyone in all of North America, I'd never forget how awful the experience was. So, I have an inkling that you might have some recollection of this infamous day. Maybe this letter wasn't one I even needed to write.

DEAR ME,

It's one in the morning, and I'm wide awake.

Before I came to Florida, I had been worried I'd be stuck hanging out at the condo clubhouse with a bunch of shuffleboard-and-bingo-playing senior citizens, but now that we're leaving in the morning for a weeklong karaoke-Bible-delivery road trip, I realize I've been worrying about all the wrong things.

Even with all of Mrs. Brackman's vocabulary words, including the extra-credit bonus ones, I have no words to describe the feeling of dread that comes over me when I picture two senior citizens, one middle-aged mom, and me riding down the highway headed for the churches and community centers on our itinerary.

So many things about this summer are turning out differently than I thought they would.

Before school even got out, Mom tried to tell me that I could sign up for a summer sports camp or join the junior summer symphony at the community center if either of those sounded like fun. But, going to sports camp when you can't even make the middle school team was like signing up for the swim team but having to wear water wings to practice. And summer symphony?

What was I supposed to play? I can't even read music, let alone play an instrument along with other kids who, not only can play, but play well enough to want to spend their entire summers at symphony rehearsals.

So, instead, I signed up for something that required no talent of any kind—volunteering as a day camp counselor at the rec center. I figured it would give me something to do while all the talented people of the world were off getting better at all the things they were already good at.

But then, after I went through four all-day Saturday training sessions, learning first aid, CPR, and PEP: the Patient Enthusiastic Positive Method of Managing Young Children, some parent complained to the rec center director that, for liability reasons, it wasn't a good idea for middle schoolers to be supervising the day camp kids.

She was probably one of those parents who sat at home watching judge shows all day and listening to those annoying lawyer commercials that tell people to call them for help suing anyone for anything.

The day camp director tried to tell this parent that there would be adult counselors supervising too, but that one complaining parent started a chain reaction that spread faster than the outbreak of head lice that happened when I was in third grade.

Before I knew it, I was a highly trained, unemployed volunteer.

This of course made me readily available for Mom's OSSS mission.

So, instead of memorizing the day camp counselor motto, "Expect the best, but prepare for the worst," which we had chanted about a thousand times during our training, I should've been learning SSRTS—Strategies of Surviving Road Trips with Seniors—or something like that. But I'm sure that's not even a "thing," because there's no way there would be any kind of preparation for the trip I'm about to embark upon.

LOVE,
ME

P.S. On my way to the bathroom after writing this letter, I saw the light on in the living room. I peeked around the corner and saw Gram sitting on the couch holding a picture of Grandpa in one hand and a tissue in the other. Seeing her like that made me

58

feel like a slug. I was so busy worrying about all the junk I was dreading that I hadn't even thought about how sad Gram might still be about Grandpa.

Gram was talking to Grandpa's photo, telling him that she was finally going on the karaoke trip the two of them always talked about taking.

Hearing that made me feel like a super slug.

And then Gram cried/sobbed/laughed and told Grandpa's photo she wished more than anything that he was still here to go along with her.

"Wouldn't the two of us have been a sight to see? And now here I am having to do it all without you."

And then she sighed a big, huge sigh that made me feel like King Kong of the super slugs.

I bet if you visited Sunny Sandy Shores today... Not that there would be any reason for you to visit because by the time you read this letter, Gram will have moved on to that great senior citizens' complex in the sky, where she no doubt gets to drive around in a convertible (probably one that's even better than her Mustang) and sing karaoke every day (probably sounding better than Judy Garland or someone like that)...

Anyway, if you <u>did</u> visit Sunny Sandy Shores, (who knows, maybe Mom and Dad are living here now), you'd probably still be able to see the huge, long, black skid mark Gram left on the street in front of condo building number two.

And you might be the only person still alive who'd be able to tell the story of how it got there, because as permanent as that skid mark is, I would bet a million trillion dollars, the memory of how it got there is even more permanent.

So, <u>this</u> letter is for me, not you, because this particular letter is undoubtedly unnecessary. But I'm writing it anyway in order to help me process the utter randomness of what just happened.

We were just pulling away from the curb in front of Gram's

building when this super tan, wrinkled-up old lady jumped out of nowhere and walked in front of the car.

Gram slammed on the brakes!

The tires screeched!

And the smell of burned rubber filled the air.

Mimi and I almost hit our heads on the back of the front seat, and I thought for sure Gram and Mom might just go sailing through the front windshield.

If Gram hadn't put the convertible top up for the long trip, and if we hadn't had our seat belts on, we would've all been human cannonballs flying through the air.

Even so, it's a wonder we're all not wearing whiplash collars right now.

(Maybe it was those boxes full of the Word of God in the trunk that protected us. I guess we'll never really know.)

Anyway, Gram threw the car into park and screamed.

"Are you out of your mind, Gert?!"

"Mother!" Mom exclaimed. "What's going on?!"

And wrinkled-up Gert walked around to Gram's side of the car and in a raspy voice said, "I just thought there was something you should know before you leave on your silly little trip."

She put her hands on her hips and went into a rant about

how her women's group was not going to donate their handmade Christmas ornaments to Gram and Mimi anymore. She told them they could just go find something else to sell in their booth at the Beach Bazaar Bonanza.

Gram and Mimi gasped so hard I was surprised they both didn't hyperventilate.

From the look on Gert's face, I could tell that the sound of that gasp had given her an immense amount of satisfaction.

"That ought to teach you to stop acting like you know every, ever lovin' thing," Gert's croaky voice snarked.

Then, she put her nose in the air and turned and walked back down the sidewalk with quick little steps toward one of the far condo buildings.

You may be the only living person who knows that if a skid mark could talk, this is the story it would tell.

LOVE,
ME

DEAR ME,

Do you know what's more daunting than a widow's bucket list karaoke Bible-delivery road trip with Mom, Gram, and Mimi?

Finding out that before you can even leave on that road trip, the four of you have to make two hundred Christmas ornaments to replace the ones Gert and her not-so-benevolent ladies' group decided to take back.

And here's another riddle for you:

What do you get when you take an economy-sized package of pipe cleaners, five thousand Popsicle sticks, a jumbo-sized container of red and green glitter, and the largest bottle of Infinity Glue money can buy?

Santa's Workshop in the middle of Gram's living room, that's what.

How about another one?

What do you get when Mimi pulls too hard on the plastic lid covering the jumbo-sized container of red and green glitter?

A glitter blizzard that forms a Christmas-colored glitter-mountain in the middle of Gram's carpeting, that's what.

(And just so you know, Gram's claim about her easy-to-keep-clean, multicolored beige carpeting is not entirely accurate. Though it doesn't show lint or dirt, the more exact truth is that it doesn't show <u>most</u> spills. A jumbo-sized amount of red and green glitter is pretty hard to miss.)

And one final question:

What do you get when Gram uses superglue without reading the instructions?

A senior citizen missing six layers of skin from her thumb and index finger after Mom had to pry them apart with a razor blade, that's what.

I guess none of those are really riddles, because in order for something to be a riddle, it's supposed to be funny, and none of it was.

Since Gert's uncharitable-ness had left us in such a lurch, the road trip had to be delayed until we could make the two hundred Christmas ornaments Gram and Mimi needed for their booth at their church's Beach Bazaar Bonanza, which was taking place the day after we were to return from our trip.

In a zillion years, you'd <u>never</u> guess Gert's reason for the whole ruckus. Would you believe me if I told you it was all because of a <u>dermatologist</u>?

Listen to this:

Gram recommended a certain dermatologist to Gert. And at Gert's appointment, the doctor asked her if she wore sunscreen. When Gert told the doctor "Yes," he called her a liar. <u>So</u>, she called him a quack and got into a huge argument with him.

She told everyone she'd never been so embarrassed in all her life, which I find hard to believe, because someone who acts like she did had <u>surely</u> embarrassed herself millions of other times in much worse ways.

Besides, it was obvious Gert had lied to the dermatologist, because you didn't have to go to medical school for dermatology to be able to tell that there was no way even one drop of sunscreen had ever touched Gert's skin.

So, if you ask me, she embarrassed herself.

Anyway, because Gram was the one who recommended this dermatologist, Gert decided to blame Gram for all her embarrassment. <u>And</u>, she decided the best way to get back at her was to have her women's club give their ornaments to a different charity.

(Mimi found all this out after calling a few of her prayer partners at church.)

So, problem-solver that she is, Mom said, "Why don't we

just <u>make</u> some Christmas ornaments for your booth? It'll be easy and fun!"

Can't you just hear Mom saying that?

And even though staying back at the condo to make Christmas ornaments meant Gram would miss her first karaoke contest, Gram and Mimi decided there was no choice but to delay our departure.

So, we scoured all the newspapers in the condo lobby for craft store coupons. Then, we bargain shopped at the Queen of Crafts and at Everybody's an Artist Emporium. And before we knew it, Gram's living room looked more like Santa's Workshop at the North Pole than a condo in Florida.

The four of us sat hunched over TV trays gluing Popsicle sticks, sprinkling glitter, and twisting pipe cleaners into bells and wreaths and candy canes. And while we worked, the *Christmas Choir Carols* CD that Mimi brought down from her place played in the background.

Listening to Christmas music and making Christmas ornaments in June was wonky enough, but when Gram and Mimi began singing along, things got even wonkier. Hearing Gram's singing voice enlightened me as to where I'd gotten <u>my</u> singing talent. And imagining what that voice would sound like from the stage of a karaoke contest filled me with a queasy wave of nausea from head to toe.

Adding to that queasiness was the realization that if you put mine, Gram's, and Mimi's talent for crafting all together, it probably wouldn't even equal the amount of craft talent Mom possessed in just one of her pinky fingers. My prediction? This delayed departure might be much longer than anticipated. Making two hundred ornaments using such a limited pool of talent would be challenging at best and impossible at worst. Most likely we'd fall somewhere in between.

LOVE,
ME

P.S. When I got up to grab more pipe cleaners from the coffee table and my hand brushed against the photo of Grandpa that I'd seen Gram talking to, I felt my karaoke contest nausea melt into something for which I had no words to describe.

Breaking news at Sunny Sandy Shores—five o'clock update—I've been promoted to sergeant of Mom's OSSS mission.

Make It, Take It must be having the crisis of a lifetime, because after about fifty phone calls interrupting our ornament-making marathon, Mom told us she is flying home in the morning, and she's leaving me here.

Funny how one of the reasons Mom made me come with her to Florida was because she didn't want me to be home alone all day while Tori and Annalise were gone at their camps and rehearsals and Dad was busy with work. But now that I'm in Florida and she isn't staying, she's leaving me in charge. Does that make any sense?

She says she wants me to take notes about everything that goes on with Gram while she's gone, especially anything that, "proves Florida isn't the best place for her."

Can you believe she actually said that?

If she wants to be a mole with her own mom, that's one thing, but that doesn't mean I'm going to be one.

I'll tell you something, because you won't tell Mom, and even if you do, by the time you tell her, it won't matter anymore,

I get why Mom wants Gram to live by us, but I think Gram really likes Sunny Sandy Shores. And I know all these old people do kind of goofy things, well, actually, really goofy things, and I sure wouldn't want to live here. (I guess I shouldn't say that because if you're really, really old, maybe you're living here now. If that's true, no offense.).

But all that's beside the point, Gram seems to be having a good time, and she and Mimi seem to be really good friends; so, just between you and me (I guess I should say, between me and me. Ha ha!), I won't be writing down anything that will help Mom's OSSS mission.

Once the lieutenant leaves, I'm in charge, and I'll be changing the goal of the mission. For me, it will be about surviving the road trip, getting back to Sunny Sandy Shores, and finishing out my deployment here in Florida. Most importantly, it will be about not interfering in Gram's new Sunny Sandy Shores life.

Mom says she'll only be gone a day or two, and then she plans to meet up with us wherever we are on the road trip. (For all I know, we'll still be here at the condo making ornaments, especially now that the only elf with any real knack for this kind of handiwork is leaving.)

But I know Mom and Make It, Take It emergencies. Sometimes they last more than a couple days, and this one seems like a doozy.

So, starting tomorrow, I'm lead elf at Santa's Workshop.

Talk about pressure!

What if we have another glitter explosion?

Or another Infinity Glue incident?

My day camp volunteer training didn't equip me for anything like that.

And me being in charge isn't going to help the quality of the ornaments either. The ones we made today don't look all that great, but at least Mom was around to spruce them up if they needed a little extra TLC. But now that we're losing our infamous Inspector #1, along with all her crafting flair, there's no telling what the ornaments are going to look like.

The thing is, the craft crisis we're in the middle of seems inconsequential compared to what might happen to us on the road trip.

My drawing of a christmas wreath is wayyyy better than my pipe cleaner version.

I guess that camp counselor motto of "Expect the best, but prepare for the worst" <u>might</u> be helpful. But I don't even know what the <u>best</u> could be, so how could I possibly expect it? And as for planning for the worst, I don't even want to think about that.

Funny that you already know how things turn out.

Is it bad?

I wish you could write <u>me</u> a letter.

LOVE,

ME

P.S. Just before Mom went to bed, she informed me that one of my most critical responsibilities while she's gone is to make sure Gram takes her blood pressure and cholesterol medicine. How am I supposed to do that? If Gram didn't even <u>tell</u> Mom she <u>had</u> high blood pressure and high cholesterol, I'd like to know how <u>I'm</u> supposed to make sure she takes her medication.

DEAR ME,

Expect the best, but prepare for the worst?

Mom's only been gone a few hours, and already, I don't really think that's very good advice.

All of us have burned fingers from the glue gun, splinters from the Popsicle sticks, and paper cuts from the card stock.

And if there was an award for the crankiest, most irritable, most frustrated ornament-maker, Gram, Mimi, and I would be neck-in-neck for first place.

Needless to say, not very elf-like attitudes.

And all we have to show for our workplace injuries is a meager pile of crooked candy canes; not-quite-round, somewhat mangled-looking wreaths; and Christmas bells that bulge more than Santa's belly.

It actually made me miss Mom more than I had that first year I went to sleepaway summer camp in second grade.

I know, I know. You probably thought I'd never write something like that. Neither did I. But if Gram's condo really was the North Pole and Gram, Mimi, and I really were elves, the three of us would be fired for sure.

After we'd played Mimi's Christmas CD six times, Mimi

sighed and said, "The Lord says he'll never give us more than we can handle, but we're sure in a real pickle here."

Gram wasn't encouraged one little bit by Mimi's paraphrased scripture with a twist.

Her response was, "Pickle?! Pickle?! We passed pickle a long time ago!"

Gram was right. At our last count, we had completed only eighty-seven ornaments, which meant we had one hundred thirteen left to go. At this rate, we were going to miss <u>all</u> of Gram's karaoke contests. And Mimi might just have to drum up more donations so she could ship all those Bibles from the post office since it didn't look like the three of us would be going any farther than Gram's living room any time soon.

Even though all those Saturday volunteer training sessions had taught me I should be full of PEP—Patience, Enthusiasm, and Positiveness—I told Gram and Mimi that nobody was going to pay for these ornaments because they all looked like junk.

"Pay for them?" Gram said. "People wouldn't take these things if we gave them away for free. That <u>confounded</u> Gert! She's the reason we're sitting here in the middle of a pile of glitter and glue like a bunch of <u>idiots</u>!"

"Madge!" Mimi scolded.

And then, through gritted teeth, Gram went on to say that she'd like to get her hands on Gert's skinny, little, wrinkled neck.

But she couldn't finish what she was saying, because Mimi scolded her again, hitting the palm of her hand on top of her TV tray causing a small snowstorm of glitter.

"Madge Callahan! Is that any way to talk?"

Funny that Mimi thought Gram was being so hard on Gert when most people would've said much worse things than what Gram was saying.

Maybe I should've been glad. Because of confounded Gert and these ornaments, it's possible we wouldn't be able to go on the road trip at all. Avoiding the trip and just staying at Sunny Sandy Shores would most likely make my life a whole lot easier, especially now that Mom was gone.

But when I looked around Gram's living room, which was literally wall-to-wall craft supplies, a road trip away from the huge mess we were in seemed better than staying back at the condo trying to make two hundred of anything.

Besides that, if we didn't go, Gram wouldn't get to sing karaoke, and after seeing her talking to Grandpa's photo, I knew I'd end up feeling bad about that.

Gram decided we needed a break, so the three of us went

into the kitchen to eat the rest of my chocolate chip cookies. And it was while Gram and Mimi raved about how good my cookies tasted that an idea hit me as hard as one of the line drives I'd missed during softball tryouts.

"Why don't we make cookies to sell at your booth?"

Both Gram and Mimi stopped chewing at the same time.

"Samantha, that's a wonderful idea!"

"What a sweet miracle from above!"

(I'll bet you can guess who said what without me even telling you.)

So, our new plan was to bake cookies the next day and store them in Gram's freezer. Then, we'd leave for the road trip the day after that. Gram would only miss one of her contests, leaving her two chances to qualify for the Seniors Got Talent karaoke contest at the Borlandsville Fun in the Sun County Fair, and we'd still have plenty of time to deliver all of Mimi's Bibles.

At this point, you might be feeling a little flutter of excitement. Things seem to be taking a slight turn for the better. But, unfortunately that sweet, wonderful, miracle of an idea and the trip being back on again led to a new insurmountable problem for me.

As I made a list of what we'd need at the store in order to

make two hundred jumbo-sized chocolate chip cookies, Mimi said to Gram, "Madge, since this whole mix-up has put us behind schedule, why don't I see if Johnny can drive down tomorrow night and drop Brandy off here at the condo? That way we won't have to stop on the way. It'll save us a little time."

Of course, you're thinking what I'm thinking, right?

Who the heck are Johnny and Brandy?

And what in the world was Mimi talking about?

When I asked, Mimi told me that Johnny was her oldest son and Brandy was one of her five grandchildren.

But what Gram said next made my stomach feel worse than if I'd eaten five tons of chocolate chip cookie dough.

"Remember, we told you Brandy's joining us on the trip?"

To which I said, "Uuuuuhh, nooooo."

And I only wish that there was some way to impress upon you the tone of my voice when I said, "Uuuuuhh, nooooo," because without my tone, you can't possibly get the full meaning of these two words.

"Oh, honey!" Mimi said. "You're going to love Brandy. And you two are just about the same age, so that should be a lot of fun."

All I could think was, "Oh great! Now, besides everything

else I had to worry about, I am going to have to handle the added stress of getting along with some random middle schooler I've never met."

What if Brandy was a Goody Two-shoes, super stuck-up type?

Or worse yet, maybe Brandy would turn out to be some troublemaking delinquent who liked to peer pressure other kids into doing bad stuff.

With my luck, Brandy would be one of those really popular kids who excelled at every single thing imaginable. That would probably stink worst of all.

Mimi went on to say that she just knew the two of us would "get along like a couple of clams."

Clams?

I doubt it.

Besides, how does anyone even know how clams get along anyway?

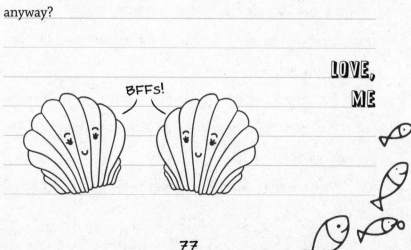

DEAR ME,

Waking up in the morning and remembering in the first few minutes of consciousness that my task for the day is baking two hundred giant chocolate chip cookies is one thing. But, when my brain reminds me, even before my eyes have adjusted to the light, that this whole thing was my big, brilliant idea and I'm the one in charge of making it happen, my first inclination is to pull the covers over my head and stay put. That inclination grows stronger when I remember that my baking cohorts are Gram and Mimi, because if their baking skills are equal to their crafting skills, I'm honestly in way more trouble than I'm equipped to handle.

So, the day began with a trip to the Friendly Frugal Food Store, where we loaded up on all the basics—eggs, flour, sugar, vanilla. And, on top of all that, we piled the shopping cart full of economy-sized bags of mini chocolate chips. (I prefer to use mini chips in my cookies, as it allows for a much more equal distribution of chocolate in each cookie.)

Even though we left Gram's condo super early, when we got to the Friendly Frugal, you would've thought it was a senior citizens' Black Friday Sale.

"Why are there so many people here so early?" I asked

completely surprised by the number of people milling about on the sidewalk waiting to push their carts through the automatic doors as soon as the store opened.

"Two reasons," Gram said. "Old people get up really early, and it's Florida. Everyone wants to beat the heat."

In spite of the crowds, once inside, we maneuvered our way through the aisles pretty quickly and efficiently. Within fifteen minutes, we stood in line to check out. But this was where our Friendly Frugal Food Store experience took a turn for the worse.

There was only one person in front of us, a shopper with spiky silver hair wearing a plaid shorts outfit that made her look like a golfer, but her color-coordinated outfit wasn't the problem. It was her cart full to the top with boxes of pasta and her fistful of coupons (one coupon for each box of pasta, to be exact) that caused the complication. Here's why: The college-age, gum-chewing, big-haired checkout girl told the pasta lady that since the pasta was already on sale, she could only use one of her coupons per visit.

So. Much. Pasta.

This tiny store policy caused the gum-chewing checkout girl and the coupon-clipping pasta lady to get into a courteous disagreement that escalated at the speed of light into an all-out heated argument. Once the shopper realized she was getting nowhere fast with the checkout girl (who was not backing down), she told her she was going to call the local news and tell them just how <u>un</u>friendly and <u>un</u>fairly she was being treated at the Friendly Frugal.

She used air quotes when she said "Friendly Frugal," and then she started digging around in her color-coordinated purse for her phone.

All the while Gram was getting super impatient, because she had to go to the bathroom.

I had a hunch the drama with the Coupon Queen was going to take a while, so I told Gram that Mimi and I would save our place in line while she went to use the restroom.

But Gram didn't have time to answer me, because Mimi chimed in, "Oh no, honey! We don't <u>ever</u> use the restrooms here."

"She's right, Samantha, they don't clean those things with any regularity. We've complained many times, but it never does any good," Gram explained, shifting her weight back and forth from one foot to the other.

I let out a huge sigh while I watched the spiky-haired

shopper getting ready to press numbers on her phone. It looked like she might know the number of the local news by heart.

"Am I going to make this call or are you going to get a store manager?" the lady said looking up from her phone screen.

The checkout girl cracked her gum and reached for her cash register microphone.

"Manager to lane seven," she said in an entirely apathetic voice.

Gram sighed, and Mimi said, "Remember, patience is a virtue."

"My bladder doesn't know that," Gram snapped just as the store manager showed up.

The manager explained the store policy again to the coupon lady, to which she said, "Look, I'm going to use these coupons to buy this cart of pasta even if I have to buy the pasta one box at a time, so we can do this the easy way or the hard way. It's really up to you."

Gram groaned.

The manager sighed.

The checkout girl cracked her gum again, while she picked at the nail polish on her right hand.

We all waited to see what would happen next, and finally the manager said, "I'll ring you up at customer service and let you use all your coupons at once."

As the lady pushed her cart full of pasta toward customer service with her head held high, I heard her say, "See, now was that so hard?"

The manager shook his head, and the checkout girl rolled her eyes.

Gram, Mimi, and I unloaded our cart as fast as if we were in a race on one of those grocery store game shows. Thankfully, once coupons weren't involved, the checker was a speedy expert at her job. She had us out of the store in less than ten minutes.

Once back at Sunny Sandy Shores, Mimi and I let Gram hurry up to the condo to use the bathroom while the two of us unloaded the groceries. Before long, I was mixing up the first of many batches of chocolate chip cookie dough. While I did, Gram and Mimi greased cookie sheets at the kitchen table and arranged the cooling racks in the dining room. Mimi had brought down cookie sheets and cooling racks from her condo, and Gram had borrowed some from a neighbor on her floor so that we'd be able to make cookies continuously.

The first few trays we baked turned out pretty rough. Gram and Mimi weren't very good at dropping the right amount of dough on the cookie sheet, and as a result, our cookies didn't all look the same. Gram's were really misshapen, and Mimi's were way too small. Not only would this make it hard to sell them all for the same price, it made it hard to bake them, because some cookies burned and others weren't baked enough to be done.

After about four baking sheets of flopped cookies, I was wondering if we shouldn't go back to making ornaments in the living room.

As I thought about what to do with our misfit cookies, I opened one of Gram's kitchen drawers looking for a clean spatula, and I saw an ice cream scoop. I remembered seeing someone on a baking show using a scoop like that to make big cookies that all turned out the same size.

So, we tried it.

And it worked!

And once we knew it worked, Mimi ran up to her condo and brought down her ice cream scoop. That's when we hit our chocolate-chip cookie baking stride, and the perfectly round and expertly baked cookies piled up on the dining room table.

And when Gram said, "Samantha, our booth at the bazaar is going to be a huge hit!", the pride that piled up inside me was higher than the highest stack of cookies.

LOVE,
ME

DEAR ME,

So, I know I keep saying, "You're not going to believe this... You're not going to believe that," but just keep reading, and you'll realize why it's even more true this time than the last time I wrote it.

After all the cookies were baked, Gram and I sat on the couch trying to guess the final *Wheel of Fortune* puzzle when Mimi walked into the condo with a tall, tanned boy following her.

"Madge and Samantha," Mimi said, sounding like she was announcing royalty, "I'd like you to meet my little Brandy. Although as you can see, he's not so little anymore."

The tall boy took a step forward and said, "Hey," and did this sort of half-wave thing.

"My real name's Brandon," he said. "Mimi's the only one who still calls me Brandy. All my friends call me Brando."

Are you thinking what I'm thinking?

Brandon?!

Brandy?!!

Brando?!!!!!

Do you have any recollection of how much I was <u>freaking</u> out when this happened?

My mind was exploding!

BRANDY
IS
A
BOY?!

His friends call him "Brando"?

I'd been worried that Brandy might be a snobby do-gooder or a juvenile delinquent, then this supercute, muscular, athletic-looking, dimple-faced, middle-school boy shows up?

I was going to ride in the back seat on a widow's bucket list karaoke road trip listening to Gram sing karaoke and delivering Bibles all over south Florida with a guy who looked so good he could be on the cover of every teen magazine ever published?

Lots of girls might think this was great.

Lots of girls might dream of luck like this.

Lots of girls might be giddy with excitement at even the thought of this.

But not me.

Not us!

Guys like Brando don't even talk to girls like me.

How could they?

They don't even know girls like me exist.

I'd learned that in the first five minutes of middle school.

No matter how old you are, you have to remember the moment we met Brandon.

And if you're reading this, we obviously survived, but at this moment, I can't for the life of me see how.

LOVE,

ME

DEAR ME,

Okay, so remember a couple letters ago when I thought that Mimi's *Christmas Choir Carols* CD was bad?

That music was nothing compared to the music I've heard so far this morning.

Let me give you a little recap:

We started out the road trip with Broadway hits, which I actually love, but not the way Gram and Mimi were belting them out.

Mimi's high-pitched, shrill voice and Gram's quivery warble—which was all over the place, yet actually never seemed to land on the right note—ruined some of my favorite show tunes.

After they massacred so many songs I adored, from many of my most-treasured musicals, Mimi put in *Big Band Hits*. She said it reminded her of her father, because when she was growing up, he had played trombone in a jazz band called Bebop Brass.

While Mimi shrieked out the lyrics to songs like "Chattanooga Choo Choo" and "Boogie-Woogie Bugle Boy," Gram, who didn't know all the words, blew air through

87

her lips to make what _she_ thought sounded like trumpet and trombone music.

It made me wish Gram had left the top down on the Mustang. At least then some of the sound would've been lost in the wind. (But Gram was afraid we'd get sunburned, so she said the top would stay up for the duration of the road trip. I was trying to look on the bright side, at least without the top down, there was no need for Gram to wear her leopard-print babushka.)

Gram and Mimi sat in the front seat—Gram with her wraparound prescription driving glasses and Mimi with her flip-up sunglass lenses attached to her regular glasses. Brandon and I sat in the back.

I felt like I was in a zany Hallmark Channel original movie about two middle schoolers being kidnapped in a sports car by two elderly women who had just escaped from a high-security retirement home.

The front-seat concert kept getting louder and louder, so finally Brandon and I had put in our earbuds. But the most expensive noise-canceling earbuds ever invented could not entirely muffle Gram and Mimi's singing. So, at least for the time being, it looked like we were stuck with the senior citizen

duet concerto. Our only hope was that they might get laryngitis and lose their voices from singing too much.

Brandon kept looking over at me and rolling his eyes as if to say, "We're both in this together, and isn't it funny?"

But, that dimpled smile of his, which would've made all the girls in my school both drool and melt at the same time, only reminded me that people like me were never in anything with people like Brando.

When we had first gotten into the car, Brandon and I talked a little, or I should say tried to talk. But I wouldn't have described our conversation as, "getting along like clams," as Mimi predicted.

"So, you're gonna be in seventh next year?" Brandon asked.

"Yeah."

"Cool."

"What about you?"

"Eighth."

(Long, silent pause except for Gram and Mimi's singing soundtrack in the background.)

"Ever been to Florida before?" Brandon asked.

"No."

"Where do you live?"

"Illinois."

(Car sing-along interlude.)

"Do you have any brothers and sisters?"

"Two sisters."

"Older or younger?"

"Older."

"What about you?"

"One brother. Older."

As you can see, our conversation wasn't exactly what you would call sparkling, which is why, eventually, even if there hadn't been all that singing going on, we both would've put our earbuds in anyway.

Later, when Gram and Mimi put in the CD of *Greatest Hymns of Our Faith*, I actually thought about jumping out of the car. We were only doing about forty miles per hour on some back road near the edge of the Everglades. I figured I could just dive and roll into the swamp grass at the side of the road. So how bad could it be?

But you know me well enough to know that I'm just kidding and that I'd never do something like that. I talk big, but, in actuality, I'm pretty much a chicken at heart.

Instead, I tried to think of ways to get back at Mom for

leaving me in such a predicament, but all that holy music filling up Gram's Mustang made it hard to focus on revenge.

I wished I could at least call Mom to whine and complain about everything, but the Make It, Take It emergency she'd gone home for had left her virtually unreachable. I'd barely heard from her since she left. And I knew if I called Dad and complained, it better really be an <u>actual</u> emergency, or I'd wish my cell phone service hadn't been working. But when Mimi popped in her CD of old television theme songs and "Happy Days" began to play, and Brando joined the car sing-along, it came really close to being an actual emergency.

The whole thing was just so cringe-worthy and awkward.

Gram and Mimi sounding <u>so</u> bad.

Me being in the back seat with a strange boy.

And now Brandon singing along.

You probably won't be surprised when I tell you that, even though it was hard to hear over the appallingly, horrendous sounds coming from the front seat, it seemed like Brandon actually might have a pretty good voice.

But why wouldn't he?

He seemed like one of those multitalented people who would've found his name on the roster of just about anything he tried out for no matter what it was. And even if he didn't make a team or get a part, he seemed so confident, he would've laughed it off like it was entertainingly amusing.

It took all my willpower to resist the urge to lunge over the front seat and eject that CD. I wanted that thing to shoot out of the CD player like a flying saucer, crash against the rear window, and shatter into a thousand pieces.

But instead I just fake-smiled at Brando when he turned to me and said, "C'mon, Sam, sing along! Ya gotta know this one!"

And then he clapped to the beat and rocked back and forth.

That was the problem with guys like Brando.

They were so cool.

No matter what they did, it never tarnished their coolness.

You of all people know I'm the exact opposite. No matter what I did, I somehow only end up enhancing my awkwardness.

Even so, you might be wondering why it mattered so much what Brandon thought of me. After all, he didn't go to my school, we didn't live in the same state, and after this week I'm sure I'd never see him again. But if you don't *get* why it mattered, you must be so old that you don't remember what it was like to be a middle schooler.

With the memory of the Spring Fine Arts Festival audition

so fresh in my mind, the last thing I wanted to do was add my voice to this kooky car choir. What if Brandon thought I sounded worse than Gram and Mimi?

So, I mouthed the lyrics to "Happy Days," pretending to sing.

And as I stared out the side window of the car and pretend-sang, I thought about how thankful I was for the garbage bag full of old clothes that sat wedged between Brandon and me in the back seat.

Mimi had decided to bring the bag along at the last minute. Apparently while collecting all that money for the Bibles we'd be delivering, she also collected old clothes from people at Sunny Sandy Shores.

"You never know the people in need, put in our path, who might be blessed by these clothes," Mimi had said.

And even though Mimi overflowed with enthusiasm at the thought of being able to "bless" people "in our path," Gram told Mimi the trunk was full, and we couldn't take the clothes.

But ever since Brandon had walked into Gram's condo, I'd been thinking about how intensely self-conscious I'd feel sitting right next to him in Gram's tiny car for the entire road trip. So,

I suggested putting that big garbage bag full of clothes in the back seat between the two of us.

And, even though we were a little squished and my leg was sticky with sweat because it was plastered up against that bulging plastic trash bag, it turns out Mimi was right. The clothes were already blessing a person in need...me.

LOVE,
ME

DEAR ME,

I wonder if maybe, with all the derogatory things I've written about Brandon, that you might be thinking I'm a little stuck-up. But that's not it at all.

(Actually, if there was an exact antonym for stuck-up, it would be me.)

The thing is that Brando is like both of my sisters and all the popular kids at school rolled up into one too-cute, too-talented person.

My reason for surmising this—besides his good looks and semi-melodic singing voice—is because when Mimi introduced him to Gram and me, she went on and on about all his achievements and awards as a pitcher on his traveling baseball team.

Apparently, he has the staggering ability to throw fastballs, knuckleballs, and sliders, whatever those are. As a result, he has clinched tournaments from one end of the state to the other. The way Mimi talked, you'd think the kid had single-handedly won the World Series or something. I was surprised he didn't come walking into Gram's condo pushing a cart full of trophies.

Anyway, the only reason he wasn't off pitching no-hitter after no-hitter this summer was because he had some wrist injury he was recovering from. The wrist splint he wore on his right wrist meant he couldn't play baseball for at least another month.

So, when his dad (Mimi's son Johnny) found out about Gram and Mimi's road trip, he and Mimi made plans for Brandon to come along.

I know it isn't his fault he's on this trip. And I'm sure he's a nice enough kid. But the pressure of "hanging out" with Brando 24–7 for the next week overwhelms me with a combination of anxiety, exhaustion, and trepidation, leaving me in a constant state of nausea.

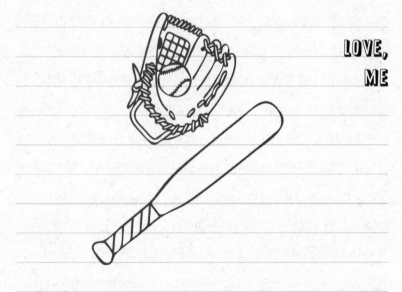

LOVE,
ME

DEAR ME,

When school starts in the fall, I'm going to tell Mrs. Brackman that I wish she'd taught us more vocab words, because then I wouldn't have to start every letter by writing, "You're <u>never</u> going to believe what happened next."

If I knew more words, I'd have lots more ways to say, "What you're about to read is remarkably unbelievable."

Anyway, I won't keep telling you, "You're never going to believe" stuff, I'll just get right into telling you what happened next, but just know that the likelihood from here on out of things being highly inconceivable is immensely overwhelming.

I'll just preface this letter by saying that I'm actually writing it while sitting on the blacktop outside Gram's car while the four of us are stranded on the side of the road.

Who knew when I was contemplating jumping out of the car, that I wouldn't even have to jump in order to find myself practically sitting in swamp grass?

Here's what happened:

Once the three-person mini-choir finished the last TV theme song (in case you were wondering, their finale was whistling the <u>Andy Griffith Show</u> theme song, which I only recognized because Dad watches reruns of it all the time, and I guess Mimi used to watch it with Brandy when he was little), we all decided it was time to stop somewhere to get gas/go to the restroom/maybe get a snack.

Gram told us she was happy to stop, but she seemed sort of proud of herself in that she didn't need to use the restroom just yet. I'm not sure why she was so proud of that, but maybe when you're old, even little things like that are a big accomplishment.

Anyway, Mimi shuffled through the directions Toe-Fungus Harold had printed out for her from his computer, but she couldn't quite figure out exactly where we were.

Brando, who obviously is used to being a hero without even trying, pulled out his cell phone and said, "I'll just figure out where we are on my phone."

But as soon as he looked at his phone screen, he realized he had no cell service way out wherever the heck we were, so I guess, even for him, saving the day isn't always as easy as it looks.

"That's why we've got these," Mimi said holding up the crumpled mess of papers she had in her hands. "Harold told me there wouldn't be any Global Positioning System access way out here."

It took me a minute to realize Mimi was talking about GPS.

(I'd never actually heard anyone say what GPS stood for out loud.)

While Mimi continued to flip through Harold's printed directions, Gram mumbled something about maybe if we'd stayed on the main roads, we'd still have cell service, to which Mimi said, "And miss all this nature?"

I didn't know what Mimi was talking about since, so far, swamp grass was the only nature we'd seen.

That is, until Mimi shrieked, "MAAAADGE! STOOOOOP!!!"

Gram jammed on the brakes.

We all lurched forward, only to be slammed back against the seats again.

The tires squealed louder than they had back at Sunny Sandy Shores in front of condo building number two.

The car skidded into a spin.

We all got smushed up against the right side of the car as the Mustang spun in a circle in the middle of the road.

When the car finally stopped, we faced sideways on the road with the back end of the Mustang leaning toward the shallow ditch on the other side of the shoulder.

Thankfully we were on a rural road, and there wasn't any

traffic. If there had been, Gram's Mustang would've bounced off who knows what like a pinball in a pinball machine.

Once the car stopped, it rolled backward until we landed in the swampy mire of the ditch with a splat. The thick, wet mud sucked at the car tires like super gravity.

That's when Gram yelled:

"WHAT
IN
THE
SAM
HILL
IS WRONG WITH YOU?!"

Brandon and I looked at each other, and then we looked at Mimi.

That's when in a small, quiet voice she said, "It was a turtle. In the road. You were about to run over a turtle."

We all looked out the window to see a turtle, as big as an extra-large pizza, lumbering across the deserted road.

"You mean to tell me..."

Gram began in the calm, steady voice she had used when battling Mom back at the condo, but then she finished in a rush.

"You almost killed the four of us because of a TURTLE?"

"Well, I didn't want you to run over it," Mimi said meekly.

(not actual size)

"It's a TURTLE!" Gram shrieked.

I totally agreed with Gram, but she yelled _so_ loud and looked _so_ mad, I felt really bad for Mimi.

Just an hour earlier Mimi had been singing, "We're Marching to Zion." At the moment, she probably wished she was _in_ Zion instead of in the front seat with Gram.

"Well, I'm sorry, Madge," Mimi said. "You know how I don't like to see harm befall one of God's creatures."

It surprised me that Mimi defended herself when Gram had yelled as loud as she did.

But Mimi's defense didn't mean anything to Gram, because Gram looked at Brandon and me in the back seat and said sternly, "We're responsible for those two, you know."

And that's what did it.

Mimi lost it.

She buried her head in her hands and sobbed, and it didn't take long before the sobs turned into wails.

Gram opened the car door and got out. But, since the car was halfway in the ditch, Gram getting out made the front end of the car lighter than the back end. So, the swampy mud of the ditch sucked even harder, and we all felt the car sink deeper in the muck.

Gram pounded on the hood of her Mustang with her fists, and Mimi's sobs turned into something which I would need a new vocab word to describe.

LOVE,
ME

P.S. I began this letter by saying I was writing it while sitting on the side of the road. This postscript is to let you know that I had to finish the letter while sitting in the car. Here's the reason why:

After Gram got out of the car, we all did. And, after a little more yelling from Gram, and a lot more sobbing from Mimi, we came up with a plan. We'd wait for a passing car, flag them down, and go for help. To tell you the truth, it wasn't much of a plan. It was kind of our only option, and it would've actually been an okay plan except for one, small thing. We were on such a deserted, rural road there was literally NO traffic of any kind.

I finally sat down at the edge of the ditch to wait, and Mimi did too, but not before putting the stack of Harold's directions underneath her so she wouldn't have to sit directly on the ground. Gram leaned against the side of the Mustang.

None of our phones were working, but even so, while we waited, Brandon paced back and forth in front of the car holding his phone up to the sky. It was undeniably evident that none of our phones were going to work way out in the boondocks, so I'll never understand why he kept thinking his would.

Anyway, just as it was becoming clear to all of us that we were going to have to come up with a different plan if we didn't want to live on the side of the road for the rest of our lives, Brandon yelled at the top of his lungs, "ALLIGATOR!!!!!!"

"Good heavens!" Gram exclaimed.

"Lord have mercy!" Mimi shrieked.

"Yikes!" I yelled.

Brandon ran toward the Mustang and flung open the door. I scrambled to my feet and grabbed Gram and Mimi by their wrists. I dragged/pulled/pushed them toward the car.

Brandon dove between the two front seats to get into the back.

Gram climbed and clawed her way over the center console to the driver's side.

Mimi clambered in after her, and before she could even sit down, I shoved her so I could get inside too.

Then I slammed the door shut like our lives depended on it because for all I knew, they did. (It was a good thing Mimi was so skinny or I might not have made it.)

The only thing we left behind was Harold's directions that were pressed into the damp ground where Mimi had been sitting on them.

While we panted and caught our breath, we watched an alligator lumber across the road from one swampy ditch to the other just like the turtle had done. And I don't know what everyone else was thinking, but what I was thinking was, "Hope for the best, but prepare for the worst" was the worst motto ever. Preparing for the worst meant I should start thinking about what else might come out of the swamp that surrounded us. I sure didn't see how thinking about that was going to be any kind of help at all.

DEAR ME,

Sorry about the mud splatters on these pages. There was no way to avoid them, and honestly, a few mud splatters in comparison to the crisis we're currently in is really quite minor.

After the alligator scare, we sat in the car waiting. For what? I'm not sure. It was obvious we were <u>way</u> past being in a pickle, but no one was offering any suggestions.

Gram was mad at Mimi.

Mimi was blaming herself.

And Brandon?

Who knows?

I mean, I was thankful he wasn't holding up his phone anymore, but he wasn't coming up with any ideas about what we should do either. He sat with his chin in his hand, his elbow resting on the open window, staring out at the horizon like the Everglade Emergency Agency would gallop up at any moment. So much for him actually saving the day.

I finally asked Brandon if he thought we could push the Mustang out of the ditch if Gram pressed the gas pedal while we pushed.

But before he could even answer, Gram said, "Under <u>no</u>

circumstances, Samantha, are the two of you getting out of this car. We just saw an alligator, for goodness' sakes!"

I told her we might have to start <u>hunting</u> alligators and <u>eating</u> them if we didn't do <u>something</u>.

I kind of surprised myself by the amount of sarcasm I used to say this, because I'd never been sarcastic with Gram before, but sitting in the car doing <u>nothing</u> was getting us <u>nowhere</u>.

Forget about sitting around hoping for the best while preparing for the worst. We were smack dab in the middle of the "worst," and getting out of it was apparently going to take more than holding up a cell phone with no service or staying in the safety of Gram's Mustang waiting to be rescued.

Once I convinced Gram it was our only option, I assured her that Brandon and I would check that the coast was clear before getting out of the car. Then we'd run down in the ditch and give the car a push. As soon as the car was out of the mud, Brandon and I would skedaddle back up on to the road, jump in the car, and we'd be on our way.

"Even if we thought that was safe," Mimi said. "Brandy's not supposed to use his wrist."

"Yeah," Brandon said, quickly agreeing with Mimi. "I gotta let this thing heal all the way or I'll never get back to baseball."

All I could think was, are you kidding me?

Did anyone else besides me care at all about getting out of this ditch before Brandon and I were as old as Gram and Mimi?

I knew from my volunteer training that I should try to be patient, enthusiastic, and positive, but I'd like to know how I was supposed to do that with this car full of naysayers.

I told Mimi that Brandon could just push with one hand, because unless someone else had a better idea, I didn't see how we had any choice but to give it a try.

So, that's how Brandon and I ended up standing in the ditch, me with two hands on the back of the Mustang and Brandon with one.

"Everybody on three!" I yelled as Gram put the car in drive.

Brandon and I took one last look around to be sure there weren't any alligators or any worse swamp creatures of God roaming around ready to swallow us whole.

Then we put our heads down and counted together.

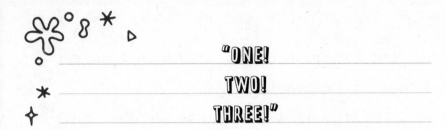

"ONE!
TWO!
THREE!"

But the only thing that moved, besides the tires spinning, was the sludgy, swampy mud that splattered and splashed up at Brandon and me.

"STOP!" We both yelled, even louder than Mimi had yelled to save that turtle's life.

But as you can tell from the mud smeared on this paper, we didn't yell quickly enough.

Mimi wailed from inside the car.

Gram yelled, "Gosh <u>darn</u> it!" and hit the steering wheel with her fist.

And Brandon and I turned toward each other, froze for a couple seconds, and then laughed

SO
HARD!

Brandon looked like a creepy creature from an amateur monster movie, which meant <u>I</u> must've looked like one too.

If it was possible to literally laugh your head off, mine and Brandon's heads would've been rolling around in the ditch.

We both doubled over until we could hardly breathe.

Once Gram and Mimi got a good look at us, they laughed as hard as we did.

And our laughter felt

SO
GOOD!

Still laughing, Brandon and I got back into the car.

We pulled shirts out of the garbage bag of rummage clothes and wiped off the wet mud from our arms, legs, and faces, but, even so, there were still streaks/smudges/smears of swamp mud remaining on Brandon and me. As we sat in the stillness and silence of our subsided laughter, the truth sank in: Gram's car wasn't going anywhere without a tow truck, which meant we had <u>one</u> option...walk for help.

No one liked the idea, especially Gram, who was almost in tears at the thought of leaving her beloved Mustang behind in the ditch, but we all agreed there was nothing else we could do.

But even though there was eventually agreement about walking, there wasn't <u>any</u> agreement about what to do with our stuff.

Since our suitcases had wheels on them, Gram wanted to take them with us, which wouldn't have been a problem, except for the fact that Mimi wanted to know how we were going to carry the Bibles.

To which Gram said, "The BIBLES?! You've <u>got</u> to be kidding!"

To which Mimi said, "I most certainly am <u>not</u> kidding!"

And then she added, "If you think I'm just going to leave God's Word lying in a ditch, then you must not know me very well, Madge!"

"Well, I <u>never</u>!" Gram said.

Then Gram opened the car door, got out, slammed it shut, and tromped up the side of the ditch to the road, where she paced back and forth. Her anger and frustration must've superseded her earlier fear of alligators and all other swamp creatures.

Brandon looked at me as if to say, "You better do something".

So, I've got to cut this letter short.

As soon as I can, I'll let you know what happens next.

I'm dying to know too.

LOVE,
ME

DEAR ME,

I'm writing this letter from the steps of Glory Bound Baptist Church.

How ironic is that?

You'll think it's even more ironic when I tell you that we showed up in front of this church with four suitcases full of Bibles, which may have been the holiest choice we could've made, but now that we're here, we're realizing it wasn't the wisest thing we could've done.

After an argument between Gram and Mimi that was as heated as the one we'd seen between the checkout girl and the Coupon Queen back at the Friendly Frugal, the four of us were more stuck than Gram's Mustang, because neither Gram nor Mimi would budge. Finally, in an effort to obtain a shred of peace, I suggested that we take our clothes out of our suitcases, dump them in the trunk, and then fill our suitcases with Mimi's Bibles. I assured Gram that our clothes would be safe until we found help and were able to get her car back.

So, that's how we found ourselves walking up the road, each dragging behind us a suitcase full of Bibles.

Thankfully Gram and Mimi both figured out how to attach their ginormous purses to rest on top of their suitcases. If they

111

had tried to carry those things over their shoulders, there was no way they both wouldn't need shoulder surgery and arm slings by the time we got wherever it was we were going.

And speaking of where we were going, we had no idea.

After the battle of the Bibles, there was a slight kerfuffle about what direction we should walk. But by this time, no one had much fight left in them, and the reality was that none of us even had an educated guess. Without GPS and with Harold's directions virtually unreadable after Brandon peeled them up from the wet ground, we all decided our best bet was to head back in the direction we had come from.

The Bible-laden suitcases were pretty heavy; so, even though I didn't really want to, I told Gram and Mimi that they should let Brandon and me pull their suitcases for them.

We lost this Battle of the Bibles

Right away, Gram said, "You'll do no such thing! The two of us got the four of us into this mess and dragging our own burdensome bags down the road is the least we can do."

I was surprised that

Gram was taking any responsibility for what happened when the truth was Mimi's turtle rescue was really the cause of our quandary.

But I wasn't surprised when Mimi said, "Besides, Brandy really shouldn't pull a suitcase with his bad hand."

Oh, please!

Brandon just shrugged at me as if to say, "I wish there were something I could do."

So, we had a lot of baggage in more ways than one, but worse than all that was the fact that since we didn't know where we were going, we had no idea how long it would take to get there.

As we walked, Gram grumbled a lot about leaving her new car behind and also about leaving our clothes and taking the Bibles, but we kept assuring her that as soon as we got somewhere where our phones worked, we'd call a tow truck and get Gram's car back along with all our stuff. Eventually she either decided to believe us, or she got tired of talking.

Brandon and I still looked pretty swamp-creatureish because the dried-up leftover swamp mud clung to our clothes and ran in muddy rivers down our bare arms and legs as we sweated in the hot Florida humidity. Thankfully it was a cloudy day, so at least we only had the ninety-plus temperature to deal with, minus the Sunshine State's sunshine.

Even so, Gram kept pointing out that all of us were sweating like pigs, which was an observation I did not find all that helpful, but I kept reminding myself that Gram's spirits must've been exceptionally low. It was true all of us were facing these terrible circumstances, but for Gram, it was worse. Not only had Gram been forced to walk away from her Mustang, but because of the whole turtle/spin-out/hike up the road to who-knows-where, there was now probably no way we'd be able to make it to Gram's second karaoke contest. That meant there was only one more contest left in which Gram could qualify for the Borlandsville County Fair.

I'm not so sure qualifying was all that important, but if, heaven forbid (as Mimi would say), some other catastrophe were to befall us, causing us to miss the last qualifying karaoke contest, Gram wouldn't get to sing at all. I tried to "hope for the best" and not think about how tragic that would be.

After we had walked for at least two hours and Mimi said, "Oh, Lord have mercy!" I thought she might be having a heart attack or something.

I'd learned first aid and CPR from my volunteer training, but I wasn't all that confident in my skills. Besides, most of our training was about Band-Aids and bruises. We hadn't really covered how to give first aid to a seventy-something senior citizen on a two-hour hike through the Florida swamps who was possibly having a heart attack.

Thankfully Mimi was fine. Her "Lord have mercy!" exclamation had come because she had spotted a church steeple in the distance. Once she pointed it out, we all saw it, and even I felt like saying, "Lord have mercy!"

But even though we all saw it, there was so much steam coming off the hot blacktop, I worried the church might only be a mirage. I crossed my fingers while Mimi hummed the chorus of "We're Marching to Zion," and we walked on.

But the church was in fact there, which was more than strange since there was literally nothing else around—no town, no houses, no anything—anywhere in sight. Once we walked up the steps, we saw a sign duct taped to the door that said, "Gone to Gospel Fest. Back next week. God Bless!"

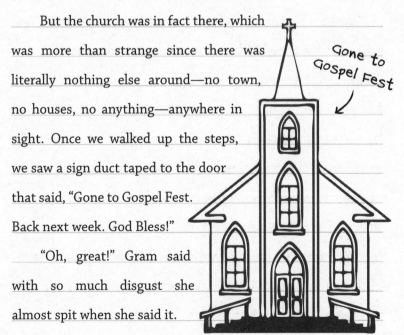

Gone to Gospel Fest

"Oh, great!" Gram said with so much disgust she almost spit when she said it.

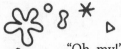

"Oh, my!" Mimi said sounding discouraged.

I felt like we had marched all the way to Zion only to find that God had left for Gospel Fest but hadn't waited for us.

As we sat on the steps of the church in the shade, resting from our impromptu Everglades hike, trying to think of what to do next, Gram suggested, "Let's look for an open window or something."

"Are you proposing we break into the House of the Lord?" Mimi asked sounding aghast.

And Brandon looked at me like he was thinking "I hope you know what to do if these two start fighting again."

Saying that Gram was super unhappy about dragging those Bibles down the road with us would've been putting it mildly. But even so, while we walked, even though we were all tired, hungry, and sweaty, it felt like Gram might be trying to forgive Mimi for saving that turtle's life at the risk of our own. But now that we're on the steps of Glory Bound Baptist and no one was here to help us, I'm waiting for steam to start coming out of Gram's ears the way the humidity is rising up from the blacktop, especially since Mimi is acting as if letting ourselves in through an open window of this church would be the crime of the century just because this is "the House of the Lord," as she's calling it.

I checked my phone again to see if there might be a cellular service miracle, seems like the steps of a church would be a good place for divine intervention, but there isn't even a hint of a bar on my screen.

LOVE,
ME

DEAR ME,

I'm sitting on the floor of the women's restroom in Glory Bound Baptist Church. Why?

I can answer that question in one word:

SNORING!

Gram sounds like a vacuum cleaner, and Mildred sounds like a lawn mower, and I know that if Mom were here, she'd tell me I'm just being a dramatic exaggerator, but you know better than anyone that I'm telling the honest-to-goodness truth. I mean, I'm sleeping in a church. Do you really think I'd lie about this?

With the symphony of snoring that's going on in the Sunday-school room where Gram and Mimi are, I have no idea how Brandon, in the room right next to it, can possibly be asleep,

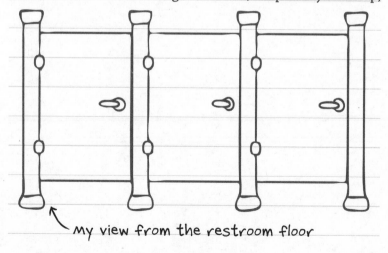

my view from the restroom floor

but I know that he is because I peeked in there before coming into the bathroom.

Not only did I find out that he's sound asleep, I found out something else too. Something that's a little bit scary.

Are you ready for this?

Brandon is actually <u>cuter</u> asleep than he is when he's awake.

How is that even possible?!

It's one thing to admit that he's teen-magazine worthy, but now, I've got to live with the fact that even when he's sleeping he's...he's...I'd never say this word out loud, especially to describe a boy, but...adorable.

He's adorable!

This trip is difficult enough without having to ride next to adorable in the back seat.

LOVE,
ME

DEAR ME,

When I first woke up this morning, I had no idea where I was. But when I opened my eyes and saw a tattered maroon hymnal directly in front of me, it all came back to me in an instant. I was in the sanctuary of Glory Bound Baptist Church.

You already know I couldn't sleep on the floor in the Sunday school room because of the snoring.

And I wasn't on the floor in the women's restroom where I wrote my last letter because it's kind of hard to sleep on a cold, tiled floor.

Instead, I was waking up on a hard, wooden church pew, because it had been the only place I could find where I could get some rest.

You might think that sleeping in a sanctuary would give a person peaceful, heavenly slumber, but I'm living proof that's not the case.

I have a terrible crick in my neck, and I feel as tired as if I'd stayed up all night long.

I never gave you the details of how we ended up getting inside Glory Bound Baptist, so I better fill you in to make sure you stay up to date on the day-to-day developments of this trip.

We finally found an unlocked window when we walked around the side of the church, and even though Mimi didn't want us to "let ourselves in," I climbed through the window and unlocked the side door of the church.

Mr. Baseball Brando said he would do it, but that was only after Mimi told him, under no circumstances, because of his wrist, was he allowed to climb inside that window. I have a hunch that both he and Mimi were just using his injury so that Gram and I would be more blameworthy than they were for "defiling the House of the Lord" with our "breaking and entering." This didn't make me feel all that churchy and charitable toward them, especially when the two of them were getting the benefits of the risks Gram and I were willing to take even though they were playing it safe.

When we got inside, the hallway in the church smelled musty, and Gram thought it felt stuffy. She wanted to adjust the thermostat to make the temperature cooler because it was currently set to vacation mode. But Mimi insisted that it was bad enough that we had broken into a place of worship, and we certainly weren't going to "squander the resources of the congregation" by turning the air-conditioning colder.

I wondered why Gram didn't argue or get mad at Mimi until I saw her adjust the thermostat later when Mimi wasn't looking, and thankfully the temperature changed so gradually that Mimi didn't notice, except to say a few hours later, "See, Madge, it's not even that warm in here once you get used to it."

Gram knew I had seen what she'd done, so she winked at me, and I smiled at her. I guess the two of us were the rebel rule-breakers, willing to be the culprits in a breaking-and-entering charge as well as being responsible for the theft of all that cool, air-conditioned air.

Mimi and Brandon were the scaredy-cats, afraid to take the chances necessary to survive the mess we were in.

But chances weren't the only thing we had to take. Because our clothes were still caked with mud, and because our clean clothes were back in the trunk of Gram's car, Brandon and I had to choose something to wear out of the church's donation bin.

Brandon ended up with a pair of pink plaid Bermuda shorts that were way too long for him and a bright yellow women's shirt with daisies on it. It was the only thing even close to his size. (Even Brandon's coolness was beginning to tarnish a bit, which says something about our plight at this point.)

You might be thinking that you would've loved to have seen Brandon dressed like that, but here's the thing... I had to pull something out of that same donation bin, and all I could find to fit me was a two-piece pajama set of knit cotton shorts with a matching top. Now you might be thinking, well that doesn't sound too bad. But here's the other thing. They had leprechauns, rainbows, and giant pots of gold all over them. I looked like a walking St. Patrick's Day billboard.

The only alternative to these clothes were the sweaty, swampy clothes we'd been wearing, which we had tried to wash out in the church restroom sink. But there must've been some swamp magic in that mud, and not the wishes-come-true kind of magic. The more we scrubbed our clothes, the more we realized they'd been transformed, never to return to their original color, texture, or smell.

So, after our church-restroom-sink showers, Mimi encouraged us by saying, "beggars can't be choosers" when she saw us in our new-old, donation-bin outfits.

I knew she was right, but that didn't make me feel any better.

And now that I'm waking up in this outfit, all I can think about is all my clothes in the trunk of Gram's car and how I can't wait until we get them back.

LOVE,
ME

DEAR ME,

Road Trip Rations

The only thing we'd had to eat since leaving Sunny Sandy Shores was the tin of extra chocolate chip cookies I had brought on the trip.

Back at the car, when we'd packed our suitcases full of Mimi's Bibles, I shoved the cookie tin into my suitcase.

(In retrospect, I realize I should've shoved some clean clothes in that suitcase too, but in the madness of the moment, my decision-making had been impaired.)

Once we'd gotten inside the church, and I pulled that cookie tin out of my suitcase and showed Gram, Mimi, and Brandon, their elation was beyond measure. In our frenzy of excitement, we devoured every last cookie.

We probably should've rationed them, saving a few for later; but we were all so hungry and relieved to finally be inside the church, and those cookies were the perfect way to celebrate. The best part was that while we ate them, it was as if each chocolate chip melted away more and more of the fatigue and frustration that had followed us down the road to Glory Bound Baptist.

And even better than that, the cookies helped Gram forgive Mimi once and for all.

By the time the tin was empty, we had laughed ourselves to tears as we relived the turtle in the middle of the road, Gram's Mustang skidding in a circle completely out of control, the four of us clambering into the car after seeing that alligator, and the mud spraying up into mine and Brando's faces.

When we went to bed, I wasn't sure if my stomach hurt more from laughing or from eating way too many cookies.

This morning when Gram found me in the sanctuary and brought me back to the room where she and Mimi had slept, I was super surprised, but thrilled, to see a feast laid out on the floor—granola bars, little boxes of raisins, mini bags of corn chips, and small packages of peanut butter crackers. The spread of packaged snack foods lay on top of a flower-print, plastic tablecloth.

"Look at what Brandy found in the church food pantry box!" Mimi exclaimed.

"Yeah, it was right there in the back of the room against the wall," Brandon said. "I don't know how I didn't see it last night."

"Talk about saving the day!" Gram added.

Now, don't get me wrong, my mouth watered at the sight of all that food, but are you thinking what I'm thinking? Saving the day? I don't see how waking up next to a food pantry box actually qualifies as "saving the day," but whatever.

"And thank heavens for my plastic purse tablecloth!" Mimi boasted.

She slowly swept her spindly puppet arm in front of her like she was showing the grand prize on a game show.

Again, I'm sure you're thinking what I'm thinking.

"Plastic purse tablecloth?"

Those three words don't typically go together.

But when I asked Mimi why she carried a tablecloth in her purse, she looked at me as if that was the most ludicrous question in the world.

"Honey, you just never know how clean a restaurant's tables really are, and there's absolutely no reason to take chances like that, so I _always_ carry a tablecloth folded up in my purse."

Then Mimi reached for my hand and pumped hand sanitizer into my palm from a larger-than-purse-sized bottle of aloe-infused, vanilla-scented sanitizer.

As I smeared it all over my hands, until they felt moisturized and smelled good enough to eat, Gram told Brandon to go ahead and let me in on the best news of all.

That's when Brandon told me that while he was in the men's restroom just after he woke up, he heard a

127

phone ringing. He ran down the hall toward the ringing sound and found a tiny church office at the end of the hall with one of those old, landline telephones. He had already called home, and his brother, Duncan, was on his way to come and rescue us from Glory Bound Baptist.

"Can you believe Brandy arranged all that for us?!" Mimi said excitedly.

Actually, what I couldn't believe was that after not lifting a finger, or maybe I should say "not lifting a wrist" all day yesterday, Brandon had woken up in a room full of food and then just happened to hear a phone ringing, and suddenly he was a bigger hero than Superman?

What was up with that?

I don't remember anyone saying anything all that complimentary when I had the idea of pushing Gram's car out of the ditch. I mean, okay, it hadn't actually worked, but at least I had made an attempt.

And who had figured out how to bring Mimi's Bibles along with us so that she'd agree to walk for help?

I know carrying the Bibles in the suitcases made Gram mad, but what else were we going to do?

And let's not forget that we'd still be sitting on the steps

of Glory Bound Baptist if it weren't for me climbing in that window.

I know you're probably thinking that I <u>really</u> sound like an ungrateful, resentful whiner and that I should just be happy that we have something to eat and that we're about to be rescued. And you know what? You're right, which is why I feel like a great big fat brat for being so disgruntled about everything. But knowing all that is not making me feel any less disgruntled.

So, with our soft, sweet-smelling sanitized hands and pristine plastic tablecloth all laid out, the four of us sat down on the floor to enjoy our indoor picnic. But after all of Brando's big news, even though I was <u>starving</u>, I wasn't feeling all that picnicky.

(And yes, I know *picknicky* is not an actual word, but it really should be.)

LOVE,
ME

DEAR ME,

Can you believe that after all I've been through in the last twenty-four hours, when I finally got ahold of Mom, she actually lectured me?

She is <u>so</u> out of control!

After two packages of peanut butter crackers, one granola bar, three boxes of raisins, five mini bags of corn chips, and eleven Dixie cups of water from the hallway drinking fountain, Gram told Brandon to show me where the phone was so that I could call Mom to check in with her.

I thought since she wouldn't recognize the church's phone number, she wouldn't answer. So I hadn't really given much thought to what I'd say to Mom other than to leave a short message saying I'd call her again later when our cell phones had service.

But Mom surprised me by answering her phone.

If Mom had any idea what had been going on since we'd left Gram's condo, she'd probably flip out, scold Gram, and send a moving van down to Sunny Sandy Shores so that it would be waiting for us when we returned from the road trip.

So, because I wanted no part of Mom's OSSS Mission, I gave a lot of short, vague answers to all her questions.

But, since I wasn't saying much, that gave Mom the opening she needed to launch into questions about Gram's pills.

"So, you're <u>sure</u> she's taking them, Sam?"

"Yes, Mom," I answered as if I was reciting a memorized line from the script of a play called *Loving Mother, Obedient Daughter*.

Mom must've detected annoyance in my portrayal of my role as Obedient Daughter, because she continued, "Samantha, you don't seem to *get it*. That medication is critical. She <u>needs</u> to take it!"

I, of course, snapped back and said, "I get it, Mom!"

"Did you actually <u>see</u> her take the pills?"

I couldn't believe Mom was being <u>this</u> much of a control freak.

The thing was, I <u>hadn't</u> really seen Gram take her medication. Honestly, in the flurry of activity back at the condo making ornaments and then cookies and in the traumatic events of the first day of the road trip, I'd kind of forgotten all about Gram's medication. But just by chance, when Gram, Mimi, and I were getting ready for bed in the church restroom, I happened to see Gram's pill container. The sections for the three days since Mom left were empty, so she was obviously taking her pills every day.

I knew I wasn't going to get away with vague, short answers

about this, so I tried to explain, "No, I didn't actually <u>see</u> her take the pills, but—"

"Then how do you know she did?!"

"I'm <u>trying</u> to tell you, Mom!"

So, I explained about the empty sections of the pill container.

Surprisingly, that seemed to satisfy her for the moment, but that didn't mean that she didn't go into this whole long thing about how it would really be better if I actually <u>saw</u> Gram take them, just to be sure, and blah, blah, blah.

I just let Mom talk.

Then she stopped herself, almost mid-rant, to ask, "And why in the world are you calling from a number that comes up Glory Bound Baptist Church? You're lucky I even answered the call."

At that moment, I wasn't considering myself very lucky, for lots of reasons. But I wasn't going to say something snarky and risk an even longer lecture, so I just said, "It's kind of a long story."

Mom of course wanted to know what <u>kind</u> of a long story.

But here's the thing, all kidding and sarcasm aside, deep down I knew that what had happened in just this short time on the road trip would've been more than enough evidence for Mom to stamp ACCOMPLISHED on the mission of Operation Sunny Sandy Shores.

Actually, even <u>one</u> of the things that had happened so far was probably enough for Mom to leave her Make It, Take It emergency immediately and rent a big, old moving truck. Forget about hiring someone to drive that moving van down to Sunny Sandy Shores, <u>she'd</u> drive it herself straight to  the steps of the Glory Bound Baptist Church and pick up Gram, Mimi, Brandon, and me.

She'd tell Gram that she had no choice but to move back up north to that nice little condo eight and a half minutes from our house.

Not only would it mean the end of Gram's life at Sunny Sandy Shores, but it would also mean the end of our road trip. Gram wouldn't get to sing karaoke; Mimi wouldn't get to deliver those Bibles that we'd just schlepped over the blistering, hot blacktop; and Brandon and I would both go home.

So, if I wanted to, I could've ended it all right then and

there, but for some reason I didn't. And even if I stayed after school for a week to work with Mrs. Brackman learning extra-credit vocab words, I still wouldn't have the words to articulate why, because I didn't really know why. (Maybe I really was a glutton for punishment.)

"Well...it's just that Gram and Mimi wanted to drive the back roads...you know, to see the scenery...and so, you know, we're in kind of a rural area, so the cell service isn't all that great..."

"Rural?" Mom asked. "How rural? Is it safe where you are?"

I was working hard to answer Mom truthfully, just not specifically or completely, so I thought about our night at Glory Bound Baptist.

Had we been safe?

I had slept in a church sanctuary, for goodness' sake.

How much safer could you get?

And besides that, Brandon's brother was on his way to rescue us.

So, yes.

Yes!

We were safe, I assured Mom.

And then thankfully I heard someone talking to Mom in

the background, and Mom told the person she'd be there in a minute.

But before she ended the call, she told me she thought I sounded as if something wasn't quite right.

I assured her again that everything was fine, and I hung up.

I stood there with my hand on the receiver and a nagging little worry burrowing like a worm in my mind.

Not telling Mom the whole truth about everything that had happened so far meant that now, if things <u>didn't</u> turn out all right on this trip, <u>I</u> would be a little more liable.

You might be wondering why I put myself in this conundrum.

And actually, at this moment, I'm wondering the Exact. Same. Thing.

LOVE,
ME

DEAR ME,

I can't help but think that if lepre-chauns really <u>were</u> magical, things would be a lot better for me right now, actually they'd be better for all of us.

I wouldn't wish for anything extravagant for myself, just some clothes that weren't so embarrassing to walk around in.

But for Gram, I'd wish for something <u>super</u> extravagant—a new Mustang is really what she needs. Actually, it's what we all need, because when Brandon's nineteen-year-old brother Duncan pulled into the church parking lot, though he was there to rescue us, and Mimi must have said at least a dozen, "Praise the Lords!" it wasn't all sunshine and roses.

First things first.

The preliminary detail I need to tell you is that Duncan was *so* cute. I mean really <u>really</u> cute! Easily a hundred times cuter than Brandon, which meant I felt about a <u>thousand</u> times more embarrassed standing around in my unmagical pj's. I know this detail doesn't really have an impact on the outcome of events for us, but it is certainly important in understanding my state of mind at this point in the story.

When Duncan saw Brandon in his pink plaid Bermudas and yellow daisy shirt, he said, "Nice outfit, dude!"

But then, when Duncan got a glimpse of <u>me</u>, he raised his eyebrows at Brandon and smirked.

Talk about humiliating!

Next came the bad news.

Duncan told us he'd spotted Gram's car in the ditch on his way to come get us, which on the surface seems like good news, but it wasn't.

Turns out if we would've walked down the road in the direction we had been headed in the car, we would've found a little town less than a mile from where we'd gone in the ditch. Knowing that we could've avoided our long trek to Glory Bound Baptist, circumventing our church sleepover and everything that went along with it, though it sounds like the bad news, is <u>nothing</u> compared to the <u>actual</u> bad news.

The actual bad news is that when Duncan saw Gram's car, he went back to the town and found someone with a tow truck. He planned to get the car pulled out of the ditch for us and leave it on the side of the road. Then come pick us up at the church, take us back to the car, and we could get right back to our road trip.

But no such luck.

The tow truck guy, who was also the town mechanic, had taken one look at the car and said the front axle was so bent that the car was undrivable.

"Undrivable?!" Gram shrieked when Duncan explained what happened.

"That's what he told me," Duncan said. "But the guy's pretty sure he can fix it, so he towed it to town, and he's working on it right now."

"Thank heavens!" Mimi exclaimed.

So, we hoisted our suitcases into the bed of Duncan's pickup truck, and Brandon and I climbed in there too. Gram, Mimi, and Duncan piled into the cab, but before we pulled away, Mimi told Duncan to wait. She dug around in her purse, took out her wallet, hurried back up the steps of Glory Bound Baptist Church, and shoved some money into the mail slot in the bottom of the church's front door.

"Can't leave without repaying the Lord and the Glory Bound Baptist congregation for all our bountiful blessings," Mimi said, rushing back toward the pickup. "Every last thing was nothing but an answer to prayer."

This wasn't exactly the way I would've described things, but

138

just as Gram had lost the argument with Mimi about bringing the Bibles with us, I knew there would be no reason for anyone to disagree with Mimi about all the bountiful answers to prayer we'd all enjoyed.

Then we headed straight toward Tow Tow Tow Your Car, the shop where the tow truck driver/mechanic/bearer of bad news was working on Gram's Mustang.

When we got there, and Gram saw her car with its front end jacked up and the mechanic underneath it with a light working on it, I thought she might cry, but somehow, she managed to hold it together.

When the mechanic heard us, he rolled out from under the car and assured Gram that he'd have the car fixed in another hour or so.

Of course, that news warranted a few more "Praise the Lords!" from Mimi.

And you might be thinking that I don't sound all that grateful when we had, in fact, been rescued and Gram's car was obviously going to be drivable once again. But that's because there's more to the story.

Are you ready for the worst news?

When I asked if we could open the trunk of the Mustang

to get our clothes out so that we could change into our own clothes again, Duncan and the mechanic had strange looks on their faces.

"Not sure what you mean, ma'am. Only clothes in the car were the rummage clothes," the mechanic said.

"No, no," I said. "Not the clothes in the back seat. The clothes in the trunk. Our clothes."

"The clothes in the trunk were with the boxes marked 'church charity,'" Duncan said. "I thought all the clothes were old clothes."

"Well, I beg your pardon," Gram said with a persnickety tone. "Those are our clothes. The ones we packed for the trip."

"Well, I'm real sorry, ma'am," the mechanic said.

"That's not a problem," Mimi said. "An honest mistake."

"No, ma'am," the mechanic said, "What I mean is I'm sorry to tell you that because I thought the clothes were rummage, I asked Duncan if my wife could come by and take them over to the big resale event they're having up north of here. My wife sets up the sale every year to raise money for the schools around here."

"WHAT?!" Gram and I said at the same time.

"Oh, my!" is what Mimi said.

"I thought your clothes were in your suitcases," Duncan said, sounding sorry.

Brandon looked at Duncan and said, "Do you think Sam and I would be dressed like this if we had our own clothes with us?"

So, while we wait for Gram's car, we're sitting out front of Second Hand, Second Look, a consignment shop down the street from Tow Tow Tow Your Car. It's the only store in this town that sells clothes. It's the middle of the day. The store's supposed to be open, but there's a sign on the window that says, "Back in a few minutes." But we've already been here at least forty-five.

You might be wondering why Duncan didn't just drive us somewhere else to buy some new clothes, which is what I thought he should've done. The problem was that he's taking paramedic training classes in night school and his teacher is really strict, and if he didn't leave right away, he would've been late for class.

I actually didn't really blame him for leaving us. I mean, I probably would've left us too, even if I didn't have somewhere

else to go, because who would want to bring two middle school-ers looking like Brandon and me shopping for clothes?

I sure wouldn't.

LOVE,

ME

P.S. One of the things I thought about while we waited for the store to open was whether someone as cute as Duncan should even be allowed to <u>be</u> a paramedic. Someone that cute could easily give a perfectly healthy girl a heart attack.

DEAR ME,

I'm thinking there might actually be a little good luck in wearing leprechauns after all, because not only are we back in Gram's Mustang headed down another rural road trying to catch up with our itinerary, but Brandon and I are sitting in the back seat with the coolest matching shirts ever!

When we finally got inside the Second Hand, Second Look store, and came face-to-face with the merchandise, I was worried that I'd be spending the rest of the road trip in my leprechaun pj's, because when I looked around, I didn't see anything that looked like it would be an improvement on my current donation-bin outfit.

At home, Tori, Annalise, and I go to the thrift store every once in a while, and we always find pretty cool stuff. But Second Hand, Second Look should've really been called Clothes from Another Century for Senior Citizens. The sections were labeled "Active Wear for the Mature Adult," "Casual Wear for the Mature Adult," and "Formal Wear for the Mature Adult."

I think you get the idea.

Of course, Gram and Mimi were in heaven, especially Mimi, who pointed out that now she could see the "blessing" of losing all our clothes to those in need.

But Brandon and I kept looking at each other and raising our eyebrows, and I knew he was wondering the same thing I was: How in the world were we going to find clothes that were any better than what we were wearing?

But then, the magic happened!

Brandon was sliding shirts along a rack of clothes way at the back of the store, and he turned to me and said, "Sam, look at these!"

I looked over to see him holding up two light blue shirts with white buttons and white piping down the front. Embroidered on the front pocket of one shirt was "Sam" and the other said, "Big B." They looked like bowling team shirts.

"We are TOTALLY getting these!" Brandon said handing me the "Sam" shirt as he took the "Big B" shirt off the hanger and tried it on over his daisy shirt.

He buttoned it up as he walked over to the mirror on the side wall.

"C'mon, Sam," he said. "Try yours on!"

So, I did.

And we both stood next to each other looking in the mirror.

And I have to tell you:

WE
LOOKED
AWESOME!

"Team Road Trip!" Brandon hooted and pumped his fist in the air.

And just like the chocolate chips in my cookies had melted Gram's insides, helping her forgive Mimi for, well, for a lot of things, having Brandon get so excited about our matching shirts, well, I don't know, it made it easier to stop being so... Oh, I don't know...disgruntled about Brandon's extraordinary coolness and his overabundance of talent. And it also made me forget about my agitation over the fact that he had gotten so much credit for being the one to find the food and the phone back at Glory Bound Baptist.

And, besides finding the matching shirts, there's one more thing which could just prove that the Irish might be on to something with those magical little leprechauns. When the tow truck/mechanic gave away all our clothes, he also gave away the bulging bag full of rummage clothes from the back seat. And I wouldn't go around broadcasting this or posting it online, but just between you and me, I'm not going to complain that there's no more plastic garbage bag separating Brandon and me in the back seat.

LOVE,
ME

DEAR ME,

Even though I was still wearing the pajama bottoms from the Glory Bound Baptist donation bin, I was feeling pretty AWESOME in my Team Road Trip shirt. The plan was at some point to find a real store so that Brandon and I could buy some more new clothes. But, now that Brandon and I looked like we were on the same team—and it was a team I didn't mind being on—getting a new pair of shorts didn't seem as important. And I was certainly in no hurry to put on a new shirt.

(With the wide variety of clothing available for the mature adult at Second Hand, Second Look, Gram and Mimi had found more than enough clothes for themselves to last until the end of the trip.)

Anyway, all of us were in a good mood when we arrived at Harmony Baptist, the first church on Mimi's list. Mimi's inability to stop herself from going on and on meant that in the first five minutes, the church secretary knew all about our travel woes going all the way back to the skid mark at Sunny Sandy Shores.

As a result, the Harmony Baptist secretary, whose name was Melody (can you even believe that?), offered to deliver the rest of Mimi's Bibles to the other churches we planned to visit to give us extra time so that we'd be sure to make it to Gram's last qualifying karaoke contest.

Mimi was so grateful she just about strangled Melody in a spindly-marionette-armed hug, and that led to Melody insisting that we all sit down in the church kitchen while she heated up some leftovers from the church's spaghetti supper, which had taken place the night before. Not only did we devour huge helpings of spaghetti and meatballs, but we ate garlic bread, salad, and plenty of pie. And while we feasted, Melody printed out a fresh copy of Harold's directions, which Mimi had saved in an email.

Mimi of course said that the fact that she had saved the directions in an email proved that miracles really do happen. But as Melody stapled the stack of papers and then handed them to Mimi, I looked at Gram and decided that miracles must sometimes be a matter of opinion.

By the time we said our goodbyes, all of us had enveloped Melody in a ginormous group hug.

When we got back in the car, even though Mimi was the only one to say something about "counting our blessings," I could tell all four of us felt pretty thankful.

Mimi's Bibles were on their way to all the Vacation Bible School kids she'd been praying for.

Gram still had one more chance to sing and possibly qualify for the Borlandsville Fun in the Sun County Fair Seniors Got Talent karaoke contest.

And our stomachs couldn't have been more satisfied if we had eaten at the fanciest Italian restaurant in town.

On top of that, I was still feeling pretty elated about the Team Road Trip shirts Brandon and I had scored.

But, about an hour from Harmony Baptist, the leprechaun luckiness disappeared into thin air, and the blessings that had been showered down upon us (which we were so happy to be counting) turned into what Mimi liked to call "trials" of our faith.

It started with a few sprinkles on the windshield, but in literally a nanosecond, the sky darkened to the color of a bruise, and the rain sprinkles turned into a torrential downpour.

Gram couldn't see the road, especially with the dark lenses of her prescription driving sunglasses, which she flung off her face just after a huge clap of thunder shook the car like a sonic boom. The windshield wipers whipped back and forth at super speed, but it still looked like dumpsters full of water were being poured on the windshield. So, Gram pulled off to the side of the road.

The hammering rain against the convertible's top sounded

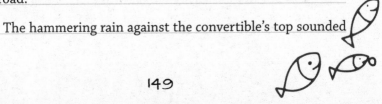

like a million reindeer hooves running over our heads. I was afraid the roof might cave in on us.

Of course, none of our cell phones were working, so Gram fiddled with the car radio searching for a station.

Breaking through the static came a storm warning from the National Weather Service. Apparently, squalls were coming in from the Atlantic Ocean, and a Flash Flood Warning had been issued.

"Oh, heavenly day!" Mimi said.

The monotone voice coming over the radio recommended that listeners take cover.

I had never really been in a Flash Flood Warning before, but I was pretty sure that a convertible Mustang on the side of a rural road in the middle of low-lying swamp land did not constitute "cover."

"I've never in all my life!" Gram said sounding exasperated. "What are we going to do?!"

I thought back to the day camp training motto: "Expect the best, but prepare for the worst."

I'd like to know how in the world we could've ever prepared for this!

(Maybe flotation devices underneath the seats in Gram's Mustang would've been a good idea.)

Brandon held his phone up against the window and squinted at it.

Was that phone really his ONLY idea for every problem?

(Although at this point, I have to admit, I didn't really have any ideas of my own.)

"I don't know why we had to listen to Harold and take these confounded back roads anyway!" Gram said.

"Don't blame this on Harold!" Mimi said. "How was he to know there'd be a storm like this? And please watch your language around these youngsters, Madge."

"My language is the least of our worries! We're in the middle of nowhere!" Gram said. "We haven't seen another car, a gas station, or a billboard for miles. This is not a safe way to travel, especially with these two kids!"

Gram mentioning a billboard, reminded me of something I'd seen a couple miles before the rain began, so I told Gram, Mimi, and Brandon that I was pretty sure I'd seen a sign for a campground up ahead.

"Campground?!" Brandon exclaimed. "What good is a campground gonna do?!"

This made me want to knock Big B's block off even though we were on the same team.

His best idea was holding his useless cell phone up in the air, and he had the audacity to criticize one of my ideas? At least I was trying to think of a way to get us off this road.

And I know it might sound dramatic, but if you were there... Okay, yes, technically you were there... But in all honesty, my idea might possibly and could quite literally save our lives.

With as much sarcasm as I usually reserved for conversations with Mom or my sisters, I told Brandon that, for his information, some campgrounds have cabins. Anything was better than sitting on the side of the road in Gram's Mustang waiting for the water to start rising so we could all get washed away in a flash flood and eaten by gigantic turtles and swamp alligators.

So, as soon as the rain let up a little, Gram put on her hazard blinkers and eased us back out onto the road. We inched down the already slightly flooded blacktop at about three miles per hour with the windshield wipers slapping back and forth as fast as they would go while the bruised sky just kept getting darker and darker even though it still should've been daylight.

We all sat forward helping Gram stay on the road, hoping and watching for another campground sign. When we finally saw the crooked acorn-shaped piece of wood attached to a post that said "Camp Wonderful," we all cheered. But when Gram

turned and drove into the circle cul-de-sac that was in the center of the campground, even with our lack of visibility because of the driving rain, we got a good enough look at Camp Wonderful to deflate our optimistic cheer into a pessimistic groan.

Camp Wonderful?

It was hard to imagine this camp had ever lived up to its name.

There _were_ cabins, but they looked like they'd been abandoned for years.

Camp Wonderful looked like a ghost town from an old black-and-white photograph.

"Well, beggars can't be choosers," Mimi said trying to sound cheerful. "We've got to just believe this is an answer to prayer."

I had a hard time believing this place was an answer to anything.

But what choice did we have?

Spooky cabins... better than nothing?

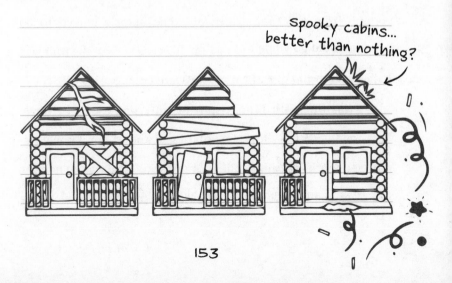

Gram drove us as close as she could through the potholes and puddles to the cabin that looked the least ramshackle. And the four of us splish-sploshed barefoot down the muddy camp path toward the cabin door, carrying our shoes and socks so they'd stay somewhat dry.

Any relief we might have felt as we took shelter was swept away when Brandon pulled open the cabin door, and a tidal wave of water washed over our feet up to our ankles.

All that was a few hours ago, and now everyone's asleep but me. You might be thinking, oh, then I bet the cabin wasn't that bad inside.

If only that were true.

The reason we had been met with a tidal wave of water when we opened the door was because there was at least a foot of floodwater on the cabin floor. Thankfully the water wasn't coming from the roof, which by some miracle looked to be keeping out the still pounding rain. Because of this, the roof was hailed as another one of Mimi's answered prayers.

I was fine with Mimi's spiritual interpretation of things, because, in just the short time that I had known her, I knew she prayed about _everything_, but if Camp Wonderful was an answer to prayer and the roof over our head was one too, I wasn't sure what we should call the water that was rising from a crack in the cement floor.

In my mind, I was calling it "the worst," which, according to the day camp motto, we should have prepared for; but again, I wasn't sure how anyone could ever prepare for the evolving adversity the four of us were experiencing.

There was a bunk bed against each of the four walls that made up the cabin, so there was a top bunk for each of us, which would hopefully keep us a safe distance from the rising water. But getting up on that top bunk wasn't as easy as it sounds.

Gram couldn't get herself up the wooden ladder, so Brandon and I had to push her.

From BEHIND.

Talk about embarrassing!

It would've been bad enough if I would've had to heave-ho my own grandma up a ladder by myself, but I had to do it with Big B.

Of course, he could only push with one hand, but thankfully he could, because I don't think I could've gotten Gram up there by myself. Once we got her over the top of the last rung, she landed with a thud on the plywood plank where there would've been a mattress if we were <u>real</u> campers and this camp really <u>was</u> wonderful.

Mimi took the bunk across from Gram, and because of her spindly arms and legs, she was able to climb that ladder like Spider-Woman.

Brandon and I took the other two bunks.

Shortly after we all settled on our "beds," the rushing waterfall of rain turned to a steady rain forest, rainy-season rain. And as the dark, stormy skies outside gradually turned to dusk and we all lay staring at the cabin's ceiling listening to the rain, I knew everyone was probably thinking what I was thinking.

No one said it out loud, because it was too heartbreaking to think about, but because of the storm and our complimentary stay at Camp Wonderful, Gram would miss her last karaoke contest, and there wasn't one thing any of us could do about it.

I closed my eyes hoping I'd fall asleep, but all I could picture was Gram back at her condo holding that photo of Grandpa and telling him about how she was finally going to sing karaoke like they'd always dreamed of doing. Thinking about it made my stomach hurt and made me wish I hadn't had seconds <u>and</u> thirds of the church-supper spaghetti.

Soon, Gram, Mimi, and Brandon's steady breathing told me they had all fallen asleep, but for me, sleep was as far away as the sunshine we'd soaked in as we had left Harmony Baptist Church just before the storm hit.

So, as long as I was awake, I got out my phone and used it as a light so I could write you this letter.

The only good thing about not having cell service is that my phone battery's lasting a really long time. And, even though I'm not the prayer Mimi is, something that I'm thinking of as answer to prayer is that I remembered to grab my drawstring backpack when we ran from the car. That's why I have my Dear Me Journal with me right now, which means <u>you're</u> keeping me company.

I'm grateful that, while Gram and Mimi's sounds of sleep turn into their nightly symphony of snoring, and Brandon slumbers in the Land of Adorable, I have the chance to catch you up on what is only day two of our travels.

Since we left Sunny Sandy Shores, it has felt more like a TV reality show/drama/slapstick comedy than a road trip.

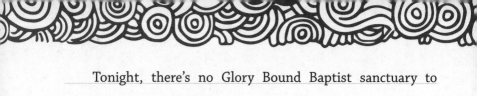

Tonight, there's no Glory Bound Baptist sanctuary to escape to so that I can get some sleep.

So, it could be a long night.

And it looks like it's going to be just you and me.

LOVE,
ME

DEAR ME,

On day one of our trip, <u>Mimi</u> cried about almost killing the four of us to save the turtle.

But Mimi crying isn't all that surprising.

I mean, some people just cry more easily than others, and you can probably tell she's kinda that type.

But today is day three, and <u>Gram</u> cried.

It's not that I've never seen Gram cry before. She cried at Grandpa's wake and at the funeral, but that's normal.

And I had seen her all choked up that night back at the condo when she was holding Grandpa's photo, but again, that seems pretty normal too.

But today?

Today was different.

Today she cried because of a gas station.

Here's what happened:

When we woke up in the Camp Wonderful cabin, we were all super thankful that not only had the rain stopped, but the floodwater on the floor of the cabin had receded. I think seeing this made us all feel confident that sunny skies might be ahead, but it didn't take long for our cheerful attitudes to turn dark.

First, just after we lifted our heads off the plywood planks we were sleeping on, Gram said, "Well, I guess my karaoke singing dreams just weren't meant to be."

Now, if I wouldn't have warned you that a gas station is what caused Gram's tears, you might be thinking that Gram started wailing right from the start, but she didn't.

None of us knew what to say about her dreams having been washed away in a flash flood, but Gram's disappointment wasn't the only thing we had to face in the first few minutes of coherence.

All of us, in a matter of seconds, realized that sleeping on a piece of plywood, without a pillow or a mattress, pretty much makes your neck feel like a twisted pretzel.

The exact opposite of "wonderful."

And while we were still coming to terms with the fact that we might not ever be able to turn our heads again, we realized how hungry and thirsty we all were. It made sense we were thirsty from eating all that spaghetti and garlic bread, but why were we all starved when we'd stuffed ourselves on Harmony Baptist leftovers? Back at the church, I had been so full I thought I'd never want to eat again. Maybe we ate so much we stretched our stomachs. My stomach actually felt like a gaping empty hole,

and my lips were so dry I thought somebody must've played a camp prank on me and rubbed sandpaper on them while I slept.

And the third thing happened as soon as we all went searching for the Camp Wonderful bathroom.

Yowza! Was that thing ever revolting!

It was so <u>repulsive</u> I think it's quite possible even Mrs. Brackman would've had to invent a new word in order to have an accurate expression of dismay over it.

But even this was not yet when Gram shed tears. You'll have to keep reading if you want to know when that happened.

After seeing <u>and</u> smelling the odiferous outhouse, we decided we'd just head out to the woods to go to the bathroom, which should've been a marvelous improvement on relieving ourselves in the Camp Wonderful bathroom. But that brainstorm proved to be impossible.

There were so many puddles everywhere, it was unfeasible to even find a place where we wouldn't be standing in a wading pool of rainwater or putting ourselves at risk of sinking in the mud.

As soon as we all agreed it would be best to get back in the car, head down the road, and cross our fingers for a nearby gas station or rest stop, a quick *bleep* came from Gram's purse.

We all looked at each other in surprise. It sounded like Gram's phone, but we didn't see how, since none of us had gotten any cell service for such a long time.

Gram reached into her purse and dug around for her phone while Mimi, Brandon, and I all dug for ours. If Gram's phone was working, ours would be too.

Unfortunately, for the three of us, the celestial cellular angels had not blessed our phones with any connection, even though Gram had hit the jackpot.

"Listen to this," she said. "Due to yesterday's storm, the Southeastern Qualifying Karaoke Contest for the Seniors Got Talent karaoke contest has been postponed until 1:00 p.m. today. Because the community center where the contest was to be originally held is currently underwater, the contest has been relocated to the 3XB on Lemon Street in Oaks Landing."

"Praise the Lord!" Mimi exclaimed. "That's nothin' but another miracle!"

Calling this nothing but another miracle was putting it mildly. Not only was it a miracle that the contest had been rescheduled, which meant Gram would have a chance to sing now, but the fact that Gram found out it had been rescheduled was a miracle of epic proportion.

Gram had gotten the announcement in an email newsletter. Gram's phone receiving this email when we were still way out in the middle of nowhere and the rest of us didn't have any service was at the very least remarkable and at the very most just what Mimi said it was, miraculous.

So, we quickly got into Gram's Mustang, not only eager to put some miles between us and all the UN-wonderfulness of Camp Wonderful, but also absolutely, feverishly excited to get to the 3XB, mostly for Gram, but also because Mimi had us convinced that a place called 3XB probably served BBQ, and "wouldn't a pulled-pork sandwich dripping with sauce hit the spot right now."

I didn't know why a BBQ restaurant would be called 3XB when there were only two B's in BBQ, but even so, the hunger that was eating away at my insides made me cross my fingers that Mimi was right.

(Oh, and in case you forgot—hunger wasn't the only trial we were facing at the moment. We all still had to go to the bathroom REALLY bad.)

What we didn't know, as we sped off down the rural road leading away from a place we hoped we'd never return to, is that we were only trading one agony for another.

(And by the way, when I say, "sped off," I mean "sped" at about twenty-five miles per hour, because <u>Mimi</u> was driving.)

Gram couldn't find her prescription sunglasses in the car anywhere. She'd taken them off when it had gotten too dark to see in the storm, and now none of us could find them. And since it was sunny again, Gram couldn't drive without them. The good thing about speeding off so slowly was that it was easy to watch for the road signs we hoped to see telling us there might be a <u>gas station</u>, restaurant, or mini-mart ahead.

Even with Gram missing her prescription driving glasses and our slow speed, the news that Gram would still get to sing karaoke had buoyed all our spirits.

But our spirits plummeted when we all heard a "ding!" come from the dashboard of the Mustang.

"Lord have mercy! We're almost out of gas!"

All I could think was, <u>Really</u>?

What could possibly happen next?

But thankfully what <u>did</u> happen just seconds later was that we saw a makeshift billboard made out of an old piece of wood

propped up against a tree and tied in place by a rope that said, "Friendly Fill-Up Ahead One Mile."

You can probably imagine how excited we all were being so close to fuel, food, and a real restroom.

Mimi's "Praise the Lords," Gram's "Thank heavens," and our hoots and hollers from the back seat filled the car with elated anticipation, as we all talked about what we hoped to buy at the gas station's mini-mart as soon as we used the restroom.

Actually, looking back now, I realize it was probably those high hopes that laid the foundation for Gram's future crying jag, because when we pulled up in front of the gas station, all I could wonder was, "Is there such a thing as worse than worst?"

Even before the Mustang came to a complete stop, Gram squawked, "What in the Sam Hill is this?!"

And even though I had no idea (and still have no idea) who the heck Sam Hill is, I agreed with Gram.

The gas station, if you could call it that, made the cabin we had just slept in seem like a mansion.

Everyone's excited high hopes seeped out of the car like air from a leaky tire.

A barefooted, skinny, shirtless man in cutoffs pushed open the smudged-up glass door of the station and said, "Hey, y'all!"

That's when Gram said, "Good gosh!" under her breath, and Mimi scolded her with a "Madge!"

I wasn't sure why Mimi scolded Gram because "Good gosh!" didn't even come close to being the worst thing you could say about this gas station.

"Friendly fill-up?!" the barefooted man asked through his scraggly, scratchy-looking beard.

At first, none of us spoke.

We just stared.

I think we were all just frozen in disbelief.

Our hunger.

Our thirst.

Our lack of sleep.

And the barrage of bad luck we faced at every crossroads had taken its toll on all of us. The customary human instinct to press on in the face of adversity had been exhausted in all of us.

Finally, I rolled down my window and said, "Uh, yeah..." to the gas station guy, who stood staring at us waiting for an answer.

I told Gram, Mimi, and Brandon to get out of the car, and they did, but they did it as if they were in a hypnotized trance.

As we all stood next to the Mustang, watching the man walk

toward the gas pump, Mimi asked in the quietest, most timid voice I'd ever heard in my life, "Um, sir, do you have a restroom?"

I'm sure you remember how much we all really needed to use the bathroom. BUT, if you would've seen the building we stood in front of, you would know how mind-explodingly frightening it was to think about the condition of the restroom inside that building.

The man told us the restroom was around back and that the key was on a hook inside the station. Then he turned his head, spit tobacco juice onto the pavement in front of Gram's car, wiped his hand across his mouth and then on the side of his cutoffs before unscrewing the Mustang's gas cap and grabbing the handle of the gas pump.

I cringed wondering if there was a limit to how much grossness a person could observe without it literally slaying them, and Gram whispered under her breath through gritted teeth, "I can wait to use the restroom."

Then Brandon asked an unthinkable question.

"Do you have any snacks for sale?"

SNACKS?!

SNACKS?!

Was he JOKING?!

Even if I were stranded on a deserted island for the rest of my life, with no hope of rescue, I would NEVER even contemplate, for a millisecond, eating something that had once been inside the Friendly Fill-Up.*

The gas station guy told us he was sorry that he was out of hot dogs, but he had five different flavors of pork rinds and ten different kinds of beef jerky.

I almost gagged just thinking of a hot dog spinning around on one of those metal roller machines inside the building this guy had just come out of. But because the four of us didn't really know what else to do, we walked toward the door anyway.

Mimi took a tissue out of her purse and wrapped it around the door handle.

I didn't want to burst her sanitation bubble, but there was no way a tissue would be any kind of a barrier against the things that were likely growing on that handle.

And it was when the four of us stepped inside that Gram said, "It's official. This whole trip was a big mistake."

I'm not exactly sure what made her say this.

It could've been the damp, musty smell or the empty heated, hot dog roller machine over in the corner spinning without any hot dogs on it or the tray of hot dog juice underneath those

empty rollers that was <u>not</u>
empty or the dusty racks of beef
jerky and pork rinds sitting on the
card table in the middle of the room or the key
attached to the <u>big, clunky chain and rusty,</u>
<u>old hubcap</u> hanging from a hook on the
graffiti-covered walls.

But I know what made her say
what she said next, and that was Mimi's
misplaced optimism.

"It's not that bad, Madge!" she said trying to sound cheerful.

"Not that BAD?! Not that BAD?! After all we've been
through so far, now we've got to risk catching who-knows-
what in the restroom of this wretched, filthy, germ-infested gas
station?! No dream is worth all this!"

And then.

Gram.

Started.

To sob.

All I could think was, prepare for the worst?

Talk about worthless advice.

There's no possible way to prepare for something that

you could never <u>ever</u>, even in your farthest, wildest imagination envision.

Then, through her sobs, Gram said, "The only sensible thing to do is to get in that Mustang right now, get on the closest main highway, and head straight back to Sunny Sandy Shores."

Having Gram cry was bad enough, but when she said going back to Sunny Sandy Shores was the only sensible thing to do, I felt like I'd just been punched in the stomach.

As bad as the gas station was—and as bad as I knew the bathroom was going to be when we took that clunky chain off the hook on the wall and unlocked that restroom door—hearing Gram say that the trip was a big mistake was worse.

And that was a "worse" I was NOT willing to accept.

So that's why, even though I didn't really believe it, I said, "Mimi's right, Gram."

Then I kept going and continued with my patient, enthusiastic, positive thinking.

"I bet once we get back on the road again, things will turn around for the better."

If the PEP method worked with little kids, I didn't see why it wouldn't work with senior citizens too.

But Brandon looked at me with a confused face and seemed

ready to say something, which I imagined wasn't going to be all that helpful, so I raised my eyebrows at him the same way Mom did with Tori, Annalise, and me when she really needed to shut us up quick.

Brandon had no idea how important Gram's tiny little karaoke dream was, but that didn't matter. I wasn't going to let anyone or anything stop us from getting Gram to Oaks Landing for her last chance to sing.

But then something happened that kind of shut all of us up. The barefooted, bearded gas station guy came inside the building.

"I kinda get the idea you folks landed here cuz a some hard times," he said, and then he leaned down and spit into an empty soup can on the card table. "So, there'll be no charge for the gas, and take as many snacks as you'd like. And here's a little somethin' to help ya get yerself back on yer feet."

He held out some money folded up so small I couldn't see how much it was.

Gram put her hand up and said we couldn't take his money, and we surely wanted to pay for our gas.

"And we wouldn't think of taking your snacks without paying," Mimi added. "We've got money."

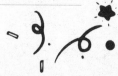

171

She started digging in her purse, and Gram did too, so the gas station guy took the folded-up money and shoved it into the "Big B" pocket of Brandon's bowling shirt.

"Betcha I got a lot more money than y'all," the gas station guy said pointing to a bent-up metal frame hanging on the wall by the door.

Inside the frame was a photo of the gas station guy holding up a big piece of cardboard. The four of us stepped forward to get a closer look. The big piece of cardboard was a pretend check.

The guy had won six million dollars in the Florida State Lottery!

We all looked at him, and he smiled, "I told ya I got a lot more money than y'all. Folks can't believe I didn't sell Friendly Fill-Up the next day after I won, but why would I? Now some days, I don't just sell gas, I get to give it away to nice folks who need it. Nice folks like y'all."

How wild is that?!

Bet you didn't see that one coming.

So, we took turns holding our noses and using the restroom, even Gram, who still kept insisting she could wait. Then, we practically bathed from head to toe in hand sanitizer until every drop of what Gram and Mimi had brought with them was gone.

Next, we each chose a package of pork rinds or beef jerky from the dusty racks, "just to be nice." And now the four of us are back in the Mustang heading slowly toward 3XB and Gram's first karaoke contest and who knows what else.

LOVE,
ME

＊P.S. A footnote regarding the gas station restroom. I would classify that bathroom in the category of "Horror." It made the Camp Wonderful outhouse look and smell like those television commercial bathrooms where, after using the most awesome, cleaning product ever, everything sparkles and shines and reminds viewers of a field of fresh lilies. And though it's super, kindhearted of the shirtless, barefooted, lottery-winning serviceman to provide people in need with free gas and give them money, it would be a charitable act to all mankind if he used just a little bit of his lottery winnings to do something about that restroom.

DEAR ME,

"We can't bring these children into this den of iniquity."

That's what Mimi said when we got to the 3XB and realized that the three B's stood for Backyard Beach <u>BAR</u>, not BBQ.

I was worried Gram might be headed for another sob fest.

At this point, even <u>I</u> was getting close to tears. We were all starving and had been fantasizing about food, specifically good BBQ, since we'd heard about Gram's contest being relocated, but those fantasies fizzled the minute we arrived at the 3XB. Not only did the place not serve food, but even if it did, Gram and Mimi would <u>never</u> let Brandon and me eat anything at a place as filthy as this one. And in most circumstances, I would've agreed with them, because although the place wasn't as bad as the gas station we'd just left, it had to be a close second. But I needed food, and my crumpled-up, empty lunch bag of a stomach might've caused me to take the risk.

But none of that mattered, because a sign hung over the outdoor entrance gate that read, "Must be twenty-one to enter. ID required."

So, Brandon and I weren't even allowed to enter this

over-twenty-one establishment that was supposed to look like a real backyard and a beach at the same time.

Worn-out, wooden picnic tables surrounded by an old, rusty chain-link fence were spread out in a big yard that looked like a huge sandbox. Lots of old people, I assumed Gram's competition, sat at the picnic tables, and there were dogs and cats wandering around in the sand occasionally stopping at metal food and water bowls scattered along the fence.

There was a stage at the far end of the fence and a clapboard shack with a drink service window over to the left of it. As I surveyed the conditions of the 3XB, I imagined, since we were completely out of hand sanitizer, that Mimi's blood pressure was rising by the minute. I hoped we wouldn't have to give her one of Gram's pills. And I couldn't help but think that if she put her purse tablecloth down on one of the picnic tables, which were covered with who knows what, she'd probably have to burn it afterward.

"They're not even going to let these kids in," Gram said pointing to the sign.

"And they shouldn't!" Mimi added matter-of-factly.

(I wondered if Mimi was like the Prohibitionists we'd read about in social studies last year.)

Once again, we were in a real pickle, and I didn't see how

we were going to get out of it. But Gram's dream was on the line, and this was the last contest. We had to think of something.

"How about you guys go in, and Brandon and I will just sit outside by the gate?" I suggested.

Neither Gram or Mimi liked this idea. They argued that they were responsible for the two of us and that there was absolutely no way they'd leave us sitting outside a bar while they went inside.

"How would that look?" Gram said. "And what would your mother say?"

I honestly didn't know exactly what Mom would say. But whatever it was, it probably wouldn't be good.

While the four of us stood at the 3XB gate, trying to figure out if we had any other options, a man in a sailor's hat with the stub of an unlit cigar in his mouth came over and said, "Four?"

And then he swung open the gate.

"We can all go in?" I asked.

"Even the youngsters?" Mimi added.

To which the man said, "Why not?"

"Well isn't this a bar?" Mimi asked.

"They're obviously not twenty-one," Gram said pointing to the sign.

"On Karaoke Thursdays we're always dry until 3:00 p.m. Only serve lemonade and iced tea. That's not too strong for ya, is it?" the guy joked, looking at Brandon and me. "I assume you're here for the contest."

Mimi, Brandon, and I pointed to Gram.

So, the man gave Gram two cards from his pocket with the number 12 on them and told us Gram would be the last contestant of the day.

"Write the name of your song on one of these and give it back to me. I'll have your song cued up when it's your turn. Keep the other card and hand it off to me when you sing. The judges who decide if you qualify for the fair are in the audience."

"Where?" Brandon wanted to know as we all looked around.

"They're undercover, so nobody knows. Even I don't know who they are."

"Oh, heavens!" Gram said.

Undercover judges?

Was that really necessary?

Then the guy pointed to an empty table to the right of the stage and told us we could sit there.

So that's how we found ourselves sitting at a picnic table at the Backyard Beach Bar with Mimi's purse tablecloth in front of us.

Before the tablecloth had even been spread all the way out, a waitress wearing a short grass skirt and a tight tank top walked over with a round tray crowded with plastic cups filled to the tippy top.

"Iced tea or lemonade?" she asked.

When we all said "lemonade," she reached her fingers inside four cups, lifted them up at the same time, and then plunked them on our table, splashing sticky lemonade on Mimi's tablecloth. She wiped her wet fingers on her tank top and walked away.

We all looked at each other and then at the plastic cups and saw little black bugs floating in the pink lemonade.

Gram mouthed the word "bugs," and Mimi shook her head. Then she took a tissue out of her purse and moved the four cups and the backstroking bugs to the far side of the table.

The man in the sailor hat grabbed the microphone and welcomed everyone to the 3XB for the Seniors Got Talent Southeastern Qualifying Round.

The mic sounded staticky, and while the guy explained the rules of the contest, that uneasy feeling about Gram singing in public made my empty stomach queasy.

Before the guy called up the first contestant to the stage,

he encouraged everyone to stick around after the contest for the early happy hour with half-price buckets of beer and monster margaritas served in mega-sized glasses.

Mimi muttered, "Lord have mercy," under her breath and shook her head.

But once the contest got started, I wanted to mutter, "Lord have mercy!" and do a lot more than just shake my head.

Here're a few details about the singers who performed before Gram:

The first contestant wore a dark-colored long wig and an outfit that looked like an old potato sack. She sang "Colors of the Wind," so I think she was trying to be Pocahontas from the Disney movie, but I'm not exactly sure. One thing I was sure about was the dreadfulness of her voice, and when her cat pounced up onstage, Brandon and I shook so hard with laughter that the picnic bench we sat on trembled like the beginnings of an earthquake. We dug our feet into the sand, trying with every fiber of our being to hold down our giggles. I squeezed my insides so hard to keep from laughing that my wrinkled-up, empty stomach felt like a scrunched-up ball of aluminum foil.

As far as I knew, Gram was planning to just stand onstage and sing, and after the Pocahontas drama, I was grateful for that.

Gram's voice wasn't great, but at least she wouldn't be doing all kinds of kooky things while she sang, and she certainly wouldn't be wearing a wig.

Next came a big man shaking his hips and singing "Disco Inferno," followed by the lady wearing tap shoes singing, "Good Morning" from Singin' in the Rain. These two contestants' voices weren't all that bad, but it was hard to get past those old-school disco moves and shuffling tap shoes.

After the disco and the tap, a tall lady in a choir robe warbled out "Amazing Grace" in such a high-pitched screech, I was surprised that all the dogs wandering around in the sand didn't charge her on the stage.

As I watched and listened to singer after singer, I thought Gram's chances of qualifying for the fair might not be that bad after all. Not because she was a great singer, but because she wasn't quite as frightfully awful as everyone else.

It's intermission right now. Gram's walking back and forth along the fence by the gate. She said she just wanted to stretch her legs, but I can tell she's really anxious about getting up onstage.

You probably won't be surprised that Mimi's over talking to the lady who sang "Amazing Grace."

And Brandon's standing near the entrance gate calling home. We finally have cell service again, so I'm planning to call Mom once the contest is over. That way I can tell her about Gram's performance. I'm crossing my fingers that I'll have something slightly good to report.

At the very least, Gram's going to finally get her chance to sing karaoke, but even so, I'm a little worried about her. I hope her nervousness doesn't get the best of her. She looks a little like a caged animal the way she's pacing back and forth. I hope she's not thinking about dropping out of the contest after all we've endured to get her here.

LOVE,

ME

P.S. Just as I finished writing, "Love, Me," my phone rang. It was Mom. It was still intermission, so I swiped my screen to answer her call.

Mom wanted to know how things were going. My answer of "fine," didn't feel entirely accurate, but at the same time it didn't feel deceptively deceitful either. After all, Gram, Mimi, Brandon, and I were all okay. None of us were hurt or sick. Our car wasn't in a ditch...anymore. We had lived through the storm <u>and</u> our stay at Camp Wonderful. We'd withstood the really horrendous, dilapidated gas station as well as a visit to its restroom. And Mimi and her tissues had protected us from drinking the bug-infested lemonade. It's just that if Mom knew all that had transpired on our trip so far, she would not necessarily think "fine" was the most truthful thing I'd ever said.

Mom told me she was sorry she hadn't called earlier but things had been pretty hectic at Make It, Take It.

When I told her it wouldn't have mattered, because our cell service hadn't been all that great, Mom wanted to know how come we were still having so much trouble with our phones.

Thankfully the music signaling the end of the intermission began to play, so I didn't have time to explain.

"I've got to get going, Mom. Gram's about to sing."

"Oh my!" Mom said. "How's that been going?"

When I told her that this was Gram's first contest because we missed the other two, Mom's voice sounded concerned.

"Missed the other <u>two</u>? Why?! I thought you only missed <u>one</u> contest. Because of the Christmas ornaments."

But then Mom surprised me more than that turtle on the road had surprised us all.

Mom said in a deflated tone, which didn't even sound like her, "Oh, it doesn't matter. I'm not there to do anything about it anyway."

Then she said, "Gosh, look at the time. I've got a huge meeting in five minutes. Talk to you tomorrow. Bye, Sam! Be good!"

And then Mom was gone.

Mom not waiting for me to say goodbye, and Mom even uttering the words, "It doesn't matter anyway," were more surprising than if Gram walked away with the grand prize trophy in the Seniors Got Talent karaoke competition.

But I don't have time to worry about any of that now. Gram's turn is coming up soon, and it's going to be terrifying to see her up onstage, possibly even more terrifying than my own rendition of "Easy Street" from *Annie*, but even so, I have to admit, there's a part of me that kind of can't wait.

DEAR ME,

My letter this time isn't just unbelievable. It's gut-wrenching, life-shattering, and downright devastating.

The last time I wrote was right before Gram was going to sing onstage for the first time, so you're probably thinking, "Oh, I bet the performance didn't go so well."

And since you're probably somewhat sarcastic like me, I know you might also be thinking, "Oh, wow, here she goes again, being all dramatic," but I think once you read this, you'll realize I'm NOT being dramatic.

What happened is WAY worse than anything you could imagine.

WAY worse than anything I could've prepared for even if I was an expert at that day camp volunteer training motto, which we both know I am failing at miserably.

And I want to warn you right off the bat.

This time I cried.

Here's what happened:

As soon as the man in the sailor hat called Gram's contestant number, she headed toward the stage. My heart pulsated as she stood in front of the microphone waiting for the introduction of

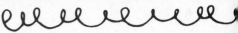

"Somewhere Over the Rainbow" to play. Gram knew the words by heart, but she still stared at the monitor while she fidgeted with the cord of the microphone. And when she opened her mouth to sing that first note, I closed my eyes and braced myself for how off-key it was sure to be.

But it wasn't Gram's shrill, off-pitch voice that I heard.

Instead.

It was a loud.

Hollow.

THUD.

And then, a collective gasp from the audience.

And at the same time, the loudest, "Lord have mercy!" Mimi had ever exclaimed.

I opened my eyes to see Gram lying in a heap at the base of the microphone.

She looked like a lifeless rag doll.

I jumped off the picnic bench.

"Someone, call nine-one-one!" I screamed as I hoisted myself up onstage without even using the stairs.

I turned Gram over and put my fingers on her neck to find a pulse.

Thankfully I felt it beating.

Then I put my head near her mouth and a tear slipped down my cheek as I felt her warm breath on my ear.

I sobbed.

Then I put my face near Gram's and tapped her cheek with my fingers.

"Gram," I said. "Gram. It's me, Sam. Wake up."

I heard a distant siren as Gram's eyes fluttered, and when they opened all the way, not just one tear, but innumerable tears dripped off my chin onto Gram's cheeks.

"I think you fainted," I said. "But you're okay, right?"

The next thing I knew, a paramedic took me by the shoulders and moved me out of the way. Another paramedic dropped a stretcher next to Gram. Both paramedics hurried to do all the things you see paramedics and doctors do in movies and television shows—taking Gram's pulse, listening to her heart, checking her pupils.

Gram was now fully conscious as they poked and prodded her. And thankfully, since she was answering the paramedics' questions, it really did seem like she was okay. But even so, I

couldn't help but think maybe Gram hadn't told Mom the whole truth about her health.

Maybe we were on this trip because she really <u>was</u> dying of something.

One of the paramedics asked Gram what day it was.

She told them Thursday.

And when they asked her what month it was, she snapped back, "It's June. What do you think? That I've lost my mind?"

The paramedics and the karaoke crowd chuckled a little at Gram, but I wasn't ready to laugh just yet.

Mimi and Brandon came up onstage. I heaved a huge, heavy sigh and felt myself relax a tiny bit when they stood on either side of me. But then, Mimi held out the pill container from Gram's purse and told the paramedics that Gram had high blood pressure and high cholesterol and that she took medication for it.

Instantly my heart slammed against my chest, because I'd forgotten all about those stupid pills. Gram had taken them the night we slept at Glory Bound Baptist, but what about the night we stayed at Camp Wonderful? I was pretty sure she hadn't taken them then. We hadn't even had any water to drink, and I hadn't even thought once to ask her about them.

Was that why she collapsed?

Was this my fault?

"When was the last time you had anything to eat or drink, ma'am?" one of the paramedics asked.

Mimi, Brandon, and I looked at one another.

Gram didn't have a funny answer to this question. Actually, she didn't have any answer to this question because none of us had had much of anything to eat or drink since our private, impromptu church spaghetti supper back at Harmony Baptist.

The paramedics told us that it was likely Gram was just dehydrated. She needed to get to an urgent care center so that she could get some fluids in her and make sure there was nothing else wrong.

They moved Gram to the stretcher, pulled it up to waist height, strapped her in, and started an IV.

"We'll take her by ambulance to Southeast Urgent Care. It's three miles north on Lemon Street. You can follow us and meet us there."

To this Gram said, "That's nonsense! I'm fine. I'll just drink a bottle or two of water."

"Too late for that. You need an IV."

Gram argued that Mimi could just drive her to the urgent care center, but the paramedics told Gram as they wheeled her

down the ramp to the left of the stage that it was their job to get her to the point of care.

Gram never thought she'd ever bring me to a backyard beer bar, but I never thought I'd end up riding in her Mustang with Mimi and Brandon as we followed her ambulance up Lemon Street toward Southeast Urgent Care.

Right now, Brandon, Mimi, and I are sitting in the waiting area of the urgent care center hoping someone will come out soon to reassure us that everything's going to be okay.

LOVE,
ME

DEAR ME,

After what seemed like a <u>really</u> long time in the urgent care center's waiting room, a nurse came out to tell us that Gram was fine. The nurse told us they needed to continue Gram's IV for a while longer to replenish her fluids. She also told us a doctor was coming from a nearby hospital to examine Gram just as a precaution. Someone would come back and give us an update as soon as they had one.

Since the nurse didn't mention anything about Gram missing a day's dose of her meds as being the cause for her collapse, my heart, which had continued to slam against the back of my chest bone ever since Mimi had mentioned Gram's pills, dialed down to a dull throb. But having my heart beat more closely to its regular thump bump only made me realize just how much my head hurt.

Everything that had happened made all the other stuff we'd been through on this trip seem like an amusement park ride full of thrills and excitement.

How could I have thought that having to sleep in the sanctuary of a church or push Gram up a bunk bed ladder was so bad?

Those things were nothing compared to sitting in the waiting room of an urgent care center continuing to wonder if the

doctor who was coming to examine Gram might still decide that the real reason Gram keeled over was because I wasn't responsible enough to do a simple little thing Mom asked me to do.

After the nurse left, Mimi told me that I needed to call my mom. She told me not to "alarm" her, but to tell her that Gram was a little dehydrated, and we were at an urgent care center having her checked out.

I was a little surprised by Mimi's somewhat "shady" rendition of the truth. Don't get me wrong, it wasn't like I wanted to give Mom details of the encounter Gram's skull had just had with the wooden stage at the Backyard Beach Bar or tell her that because Gram's dehydration was so bad she was hooked up to an IV. I just would've thought that with Mimi's undying commitment to delivering the truth to all those churches (in the form of Bibles) that she would've been a little more forthright in encouraging me to deliver a more detailed version of the truth to Mom about Gram.

I went outside the waiting room door and stood in an alcove under the shade of an awning to call Mom. I wasn't even sure Mom would answer her phone, since when I had talked to her earlier, she had been dashing off to an all-important Make It, Take It meeting.

I took a few deep breaths and thought of the time in first grade when I had slept over at a friend's house for the first time, and because I'd gotten homesick, I called Mom. I remembered how as soon as I heard Mom's voice, I'd started to cry. I hoped that I wouldn't burst into tears that same way today, I'd never convince Mom that Gram was okay if I started the phone call by blubbering hysterically like a six-year-old.

I swiped my phone screen, pressed Mom's number, and waited.

"Hey, Samantha!"

It was Dad.

I wondered if in all my stress, I'd called Dad by mistake.

"Dad?" I asked.

"Yep, it's me," he said.

"I was trying to call Mom. Did I call you by mistake?"

Let me pause a minute here. Remember how I told you that I wasn't going to keep writing "You're never going to believe what happened next?"

Well, if I was still writing things like that, right now, I'd write "You're never going to believe what happened next," but I'd write it like this: **"YOU'RE NEVER GOING TO BELIEVE WHAT HAPPENED NEXT!!!!!!!!!!!!!!"**

Let me continue.

"No, I've got Mom's phone because, well, because, well... I'll start by saying that Mom's okay. I'm with her, and basically the whole thing was a false alarm."

What was Dad talking about?

"They thought it was a heart attack, so she's in the ER—"

"WHAT?!" I shrieked.

And then I blubbered in hyperhysteria.

Dad tried to calm me down.

And through the hysteria, I heard Dad continue telling me about Mom.

"But her heart is fine... They've done lots of tests... They didn't find anything."

But all I could think was if that was true, why was Mom in the hospital?

Dad finished by saying that the doctor decided that Mom had had an anxiety attack.

Are you thinking what I'm thinking?

Anxiety attack?!

I was the one who should be having an anxiety attack.

In fact, at that moment, I thought I might actually be having one.

Dad told me that he had just walked outside the emergency

room so that he could call me while the nurses finished their release paperwork with Mom.

At that moment, I wished more than anything in the world that I wasn't in Florida so that I could be at the hospital with Mom and Dad right now.

"Are Tori and Annalise there?"

"No, I haven't even talked to them yet. Tori's at an all-day tournament, and Annalise had a lesson and then a double rehearsal. Once I knew Mom was okay, I just decided I'd talk to them both tonight at home. No reason to worry them when there's really nothing to worry about."

Well, again, I'm sure you're thinking what I'm thinking. The only way there'd be nothing to worry about was if when I called Mom, she had answered her phone instead of Dad. Or better yet, if Mom hadn't answered at all because she was still busy in one of her important, epically long meetings.

Dad told me that the doctor recommended that Mom stop working so many long hours, because that was likely where all the stress was coming from. And that stress probably caused the anxiety attack. The doctor suggested that Mom take some time to rest and relax, but other than that, he said, Mom was fine.

"So, how's it going down there?" Dad asked sounding nonchalant as he changed the subject.

Oh, yeah.

Great question.

How are things going down here?

Well, let's see, I just stepped outside to call Mom to tell her about Gram. But instead of being able to do that, and possibly get a little encouragement from her to help me face the many obstacles I've been encountering, I find out that Mom is so stressed out about her life that she wound up in the hospital.

I didn't see how telling Dad about Gram was going to help the situation, so I said, "Everything's fine."

I'm sure you'd agree that I didn't really have a choice but to elaborate on Mimi's "stretching of the truth" by eliminating the details of our most current plight. I couldn't risk passing off any of my anxiety to Dad, or he might wind up in the hospital next.

I couldn't bear it if something was wrong with Gram, Mom, and Dad.

Dad said he was glad that everything was fine, and then he said Gram was lucky to have me down in Florida with her.

All I could think was that Gram would've been luckier if someone more responsible than me were down here with her.

Dad said that Mom had told him all about the whole widow's bucket list karaoke road trip, so he asked me how everything was going with that.

I told him that so far it had been a real adventure.

I figured that at least that response wasn't a lie.

"Can't wait to hear all about it when you get home," Dad said. "I know Mom'll want to hear every last detail."

When I asked if I could talk to Mom, he told me that the nurses were keeping her busy filling out forms.

"But I'll be sure she calls you tomorrow," Dad said.

Then he told me that it was probably best not to tell Gram about Mom.

"No reason to cause concern when there's no reason for it."

Oh, no, of course not, I thought to myself. (I'm sure I don't have to mention how sarcastically I said that to myself.)

But then, when Dad told me he loved me, and that Mom did too, I realized that, under certain circumstances, even Dad's voice had the power to melt me into a puddle of tears the way Mom's had during that first-grade sleepover phone call. I took a super deep breath, held it a second, and let it seep out slowly so that not one single piece of the lump in my throat leaked out with it.

Dad told me one last time not to worry, and then he ended the call.

I stood staring at my phone screen thinking about how impossible it was going to be to not worry about Mom.

Because of all the snarky and sarcastic things I'd said to her in the last couple weeks, it was inconceivable that I would ever feel like anything other than the King Kong of slugs. I had to face the fact that I had acted like the ugliest, most revolting, nastiest, most hideous slug that had ever slimed its way across the floor.

I'm writing all this while I sit in the urgent care center waiting room, hoping that very soon someone will come and tell us some more reassuring news about Gram or that maybe even Gram herself will walk out into the waiting room looking even better than she had looked on the day Mom and I arrived in Florida and she had surprised us with her new Mustang.

Mimi's over in the corner of the waiting room with her eyes closed and her lips moving silently.

I know it's important to talk to God in times like this, especially for people like Mimi, and it's not that I don't appreciate her prayers, but I could kind of use someone to talk to.

I can't talk to Brandon, because ever since he found a Wiffle ball in the waiting room's toy bin, he's been tossing it up in the air with his left hand while pacing back and forth across the room.

I'm thankful my letters to you are helping me sort of feel like I have someone to confide in, because without them, I wouldn't have any way to vent all the consternation and culpability swirling around inside me right now.

I was already wondering if Gram's collapsing was my fault.

And now I'm wondering if Mom's stress wasn't only because of work.

Was it partly because of me?

Was it <u>all</u> because of me?

All the things we've gone through so far on this trip feel like big rocks rolling down a hill straight for me. In order to survive, I've had to keep jumping out of the way.

But this new stuff with Gram and Mom isn't just rocks rolling down a hill; this new stuff is like boulders barreling down a mountain like they've been shot out of a cannon.

And the tight feeling in my chest that's squeezing my hammering heart makes me feel like those boulders are flattening me worse than Gram's Mustang would've flattened that turtle if Mimi hadn't yelled, "Stop!"

LOVE,
ME

DEAR ME,

After a long trip to the urgent care center's waiting room bathroom, where I splashed water on my face so that no one could tell that I'd been crying, I came back to find Gram sitting out in the waiting room next to Mimi.

And when I saw Mimi's twig-like fingers holding on to Gram's forearm, I worried that Gram had come out and told Mimi that the doctor had told her something was seriously wrong with her, but then I heard Mimi say, "You shouldn't feel down about it, Madge. At least you tried."

It didn't sound like they were talking about Gram's health, and my relief allowed me to let go of a microscopic amount of the tightness in my chest.

Neither Mimi nor Gram saw me standing at the edge of the waiting room, so I stayed still and listened.

"But I wasn't just doing this for me," Gram said. "I was doing it for Martin too, but it was silly of me to think I could do this without him."

And then Gram started to cry, and when she did, a tidal wave of sadness smashed against my heart and cracked it in two like it was a Styrofoam surfboard.

Through her tears, Gram told Mimi that she didn't know why she thought doing all this would make her miss Grandpa less. She said she had thought it might help her get over him being gone, but it had actually made her miss him even more.

Through the tears that made a mess of my just-cleaned face, I watched as Mimi rubbed Gram's arm and heard her tell Gram, "You're being too hard on yourself. When I lost Herm, I didn't know how I'd <u>ever</u> keep going. I just missed him so much, but with time, the Lord comforted me."

Mimi told Gram the same would happen for her. It would just take some time.

"But you probably didn't act like a <u>darned</u> fool like I've been doing," Gram said.

"Driving around in a Mustang, traveling all over the state, thinking I could stand up and sing in front of people."

"But Madge," Mimi said as she handed Gram a tissue. "Look at what your adventurous spirit's done for all of us. This has been the trip of a lifetime! We've crammed more chaos, catastrophe, laughter, and fun into three days than I'd ever thought possible."

Gram blew her nose and laughed.

Now that tidal wave inside me swirled around, mixing my sadness with sentimental feelings I'd never ever felt before.

"Who else can say they took a trip through the back roads of Florida, landed in a ditch, slept in a church, donated all their clothes to a rummage sale, slept in a ramshackle cabin in the middle of a flash flood, and survived the worst public restroom since indoor plumbing was invented and lived to tell about it?" asked Mimi.

Gram's shoulders shook as her tears turned into unstoppable, contagious laughter.

Mimi leaned back and laughed too. Finally, she put her hand on her skinny stomach, sighed, and said, "And I don't know about you, but the time I've gotten to spend with Brandy and getting to know Sam has been some of the best moments of my entire life, and when you're as old as the two of us, that's saying a lot."

Now the tidal wave wasn't just inside me, it came gushing out in a waterfall/explosion/flash flood of sobs and tears.

"Oh, I know," Gram said, her laughter turning into sobs again. "It's just been so darn fun being with those kids, hasn't it?"

"Nothing but a blessing in the middle of a mountain of mayhem," Mimi said, laughing and crying all at the same time.

By this time, through my flooded waterfall of emotion, I was hiccupping loudly, so Gram and Mimi noticed me standing at the edge of the waiting room. They put out their arms and called me over to them. And the three of us sat there blubbering and laughing while smearing sloppy tears all over our faces.

Brandon had been outside calling home, and when he came back in and saw the three of us huddled together in a heap of tears, I think he thought Gram might be dying.

Though it wasn't a nice thing to do, the look of distress on his face made Gram, Mimi, and I crack up in such a fit of laughter that Brandon couldn't tell if we were laughing or crying, so he didn't know _what_ to do.

Finally, when the three of us caught our breath enough to talk, we assured him that everything was okay.

I'm writing this letter to keep you up to date while Gram is filling out the rest of the urgent care center's discharge paperwork so we can leave. Mimi's outside giving Harold a call, hopefully not getting any more back-road driving directions, and Brandon's at the mini-mart next door to the urgent care center buying us plenty of water to drink as well as some car snacks.

(Hopefully not a single bag of pork rinds or package of beef jerky.)

I'm sitting in the corner of the waiting room writing, because even though this last half hour has been full of a roller coaster of emotions that I never saw coming, and even though some of those emotions were more than a little arduous, I have to admit that I don't want to forget even one detail of what just happened.

I warned you not to expect this Dear Me Journal to be chock-full of cherish-worthy memories, but I may have been mistaken about that. Maybe "chock-full" isn't the word I'd use, but there'll definitely be more than a few cherish-worthy moments I won't want to forget. And I know that I'll be thankful I wrote them down so that we get to keep them forever.

LOVE,
ME

DEAR ME,

This past year, I had so many days when I came home from school after a horrible tryout or audition and baked a big batch of chocolate chip cookies. On those days, I always felt like things were as bad as they could get.

Losing my chance to play tennis or be in the play or sing in fine arts, especially if I'd made a fool of myself trying, seemed like such a big deal.

But a batch of chocolate chip cookies could never fix all the stuff that happened today, or maybe I should say, all the stuff that could've happened.

The truth is, I could bake cookies for the rest of my life, and it would never be enough therapy for me to feel better about losing what I might've lost.

Maybe Mom's right.

Maybe I am a little too dramatic.

I guess when real drama happens, it makes the made-up drama seem pretty inconsequential.

LOVE,
ME

DEAR ME,

Once we left Southeast Urgent Care, Gram insisted we put aside Harold's rural route directions. With the help of GPS, we headed straight toward the nearest main highway in search of a decent hotel to spend the night. We hit the jackpot at exit 16, when we found the Shady Palm Tree Travel Lodge. Mimi said it looked clean, Gram said it looked safe, and they both thought eighty-nine dollars a night was a fair price.

We checked into two adjoining rooms, and then Brandon and I walked to the Stretch Your Dollar Store directly behind the hotel in search of something new to wear.

Thankfully, at Stretch Your Dollar Brandon and I found plenty of gym shorts and T-shirts to choose from. The store even had socks and underwear, which, as you can imagine, we needed pretty badly by now. And you might be thinking, "Man, how embarrassing to shop for this kind of stuff with Brandon." And if you would've told me just a couple days ago that I'd stand next to Brandon at a store and pay for new socks and under-wear without giving it a second thought, I would've thought you were loonier than some of Gram's Sunny Sandy Shores neighbors. But I guess being on the road with someone and going through everything we'd gone through really changes a person.

After long, hot showers, we all put on our new clothes (Gram and Mimi wore another of their new outfits from their Second Hand, Second Look spending spree) and walked to a restaurant right next door to the Shady Palm called Meat and Eat, where we ordered tons of food: meat loaf, pot roast, chili, corn bread, and lots of sweet potato fries. We had our waitress put all the food in the middle of the table, so we could dig in and share everything at the same time. And we ate and ate and ate, only talking to make comments like:

yessss

"I've never tasted meat loaf as juicy as this."

"I wish the pot roast I made turned out this tender."

"I never knew I liked chili so much."

"I'm going to start making corn bread when I get home."

Eventually our appetites dwindled to nothing, and we all sat back with a sigh, our stomachs finally satisfied. But then the disappointment set in. Gram was out of chances. Her karaoke dream was dead. Realizing the depths of this distressful reality led to a colossal conversation about skipping the fair altogether and just heading back to Sunny Sandy Shores in the morning.

Gram said since she didn't qualify for the karaoke contest anyway, she didn't see the point in going.

"The only thing is, my GPS says Borlandsville is less than an hour from here," Brandon said.

"It seems a shame to turn back now when we've come so far," Mimi added.

I looked over at Gram. I knew her disappointment must feel heavier than a backpack full of bricks. I of all people could relate to why she wasn't in much of a fair-going mood.

When Gram had first told Mom and me about the road trip, I hadn't necessarily had my heart set on going to the fair, but now it seemed like such a bummer to end the trip by skipping it. Maybe once Gram got to the fair, she'd surprise herself and have a good time after all. Besides, not going at all wasn't going to change the fact that Gram didn't get to sing karaoke.

We finally decided to take a vote.

Turned out, it was three to one—Mimi, Brandon, and me against Gram.

So, it was settled, a few days at the fair before heading

back across the state to Sunny Sandy Shores became our plan. And even more surprising than the absence of embarrassment when buying socks and underwear at the Stretch Your Dollar with Brandon was the excitement and relief I felt knowing that our trip wouldn't be cut short by going back to Sunny Sandy Shores early.

LOVE,
ME

P.S. We ended up finding Gram's prescription driving sunglasses as we were getting into the car after Gram's visit to the urgent care center. They must've fallen on the floor of the Mustang and had somehow gotten stepped on. We all decided it probably happened during the rainstorm when we dashed out of the car heading for the cover of the camp cabin. It was just another wonderful memory we had from our session at Camp Wonderful.

So, once we got to the Shady Palm Tree, Gram called her eye doctor; she asked him to overnight a new pair of prescription sunglasses to her at the hotel.

"Makes me sick to pay full price for a new pair. I got such

a good deal on that other pair," Gram said. "And the charge for rushed delivery might as well be highway robbery."

But it was a price she was willing to pay, and I was thankful, because if we had to let Mimi drive us all the way back to Sunny Sandy Shores at twenty-five miles per hour, Brandon and I might be close to retirement age by the time we got there.

P.P.S. Gram may not have gotten her way about going to the fair, but she told us that under "no circumstances" would we be driving to the fair <u>or</u> back to the condo via the back roads. She said <u>she</u> would be driving, so it would be highway all the way.

DEAR ME,

We came to the long line of cars way before we saw the big grassy field that was being used as a parking lot. Once we were close enough to see the field, we also saw the line of cars snaking its way in and out of orange cones as fairground workers waved flags directing people where to park. I had been to carnivals in the mall parking lot, and our town had a Centennial Fair once to celebrate its history, but the size of the Borlandsville Fun in the Sun County Fair blew those things out of the water.

After following the flag-wavers for at least fifteen minutes in and out of the orange cones, Gram finally pulled the Mustang into our parking spot. We followed the crowds toward the entrance. And, even though Gram hadn't gotten to sing karaoke on this trip, when we walked underneath that huge "Welcome to the Borlandsville Fun in the Sun County Fair" sign, it felt like the crowning moment of our trip.

I could tell even Gram was glad to be there.

The smell of fried dough, hot dogs, and chocolate filled the air. It made me hungry even though Brandon and I had made and eaten three huge waffles apiece just before we checked out of the Shady Palm Tree Travel Lodge. Maybe I was still making up for the meals we'd missed.

Carnival workers yelled from their game booths trying to get people to "Step right up!" and "Win a prize!" And just beyond the games, booths, and prizes was the competition tent and picnic area. And at the far end of the fairgrounds were the amusement park rides.

Gram told Brandon and me that later we could go off on our own, but that first, we'd walk around together to check out what there was to do and see.

As we walked, Mimi pointed to all the food she wanted to buy.

"Ooh, that fried dough smells divine! And look at that caramel apple over there! Why, it's as big as a softball! But I'll be starting with one of those giant turkey legs," she said pointing to a guy in a tank top with BBQ sauce all over his face.

To which I said, "Ewww!"

Fried dough and caramel apples, YES! But those turkey legs?! Talk about disgusting!

Mimi told me they were delicious and said that I should

try one, but I wasn't interested in expanding my fairground food favorites. There were plenty of foods for sale that I already knew I loved.

(I sure hope I don't grow up to love those turkey legs, because if I do, you're probably smirking as you read this.)

Once we'd made it past all the food booths, Brandon said, "Hey, look at this!"

He pointed to a big whiteboard to the left of the competition tent. The board listed all the contests going on at the fair. The third one from the top was the Seniors Got Talent karaoke contest. It had an asterisk by it, like most of the other performance-type contests did, which signified that a qualifying performance was required.

I looked over at Gram and saw her take a deep breath and sigh.

I wondered if she felt like I did every time a team roster was posted outside the middle school office after a tryout. And the twinge that I got in my own stomach made me wonder if I'd be able to eat anything at the fair after all.

Gram probably felt like a failure, and I knew exactly how that felt. This is exactly why Gram had voted not to come to the fair.

She was only here because of us, and now Brandon had to call us over to look at the list of contests.

What was wrong with him?

"Hey, Samantha," Brandon said. "Look at number ten. There's a baking contest. You should totally sign up and make your chocolate chip cookies."

Mimi and Gram jumped right in.

"Oh, he's right, Samantha! Those cookies you make are heavenly!"

"You'd be sure to win a prize!"

"I don't know..." I said.

Thinking about entering my chocolate chip cookies in a baking contest made that twinge in my stomach turn into full blown nausea, and it made me wonder if eating all those hotel waffles had been such a good idea.

Maybe you're thinking that I was acting a little coy and modest, but really I wasn't.

And maybe it's hard for you to believe me when I say I really didn't want to enter this contest.

But it's the honest truth.

I'm not exactly sure why, except that maybe I was finally just done putting myself out there, when, for me, the possibility of failing was much greater than the possibility of succeeding.

I mean, yeah, everybody <u>said</u> my cookies were amazing, but entering them in a contest meant having someone judge them, which meant there was the chance that someone could deem them not all that great.

It was also possible that having someone like Brandon around to witness me competing when there was so much potential to fail was a risk that I wasn't all that excited about taking.

And besides that, in the very unlikely event that I somehow managed to commandeer some type of prize or award, how would that make Gram feel?

But as I played all this reasoning over in my head while the fairground crowds swirled around me, Brandon grabbed a sheet of paper outlining the baking contest rules from a pocket attached to the edge of the whiteboard and shoved them at me. Then he grabbed the marker hanging from a string attached to the baking contest sign-up sheet and wrote down my name.

When I tried to object, Gram said, "Sam, if I can't be in the karaoke contest, you entering the baking contest will be the next best thing. Do it for me!"

This time, I was outnumbered.

It looked like I'd be baking a batch of my chocolate chip cookies for the Borlandsville Fun in the Sun County Fair baking contest judges.

I sure hoped that the one thing that had helped me get over so many of my life's failures didn't become my next big blunder.

Once I was all signed up, Mimi said she needed to use the restroom, so she and Gram went to find one. While Brandon and I waited in front of the big whiteboard for them to come back, he looked over the baking contest rules, reading some of them aloud. When he got to the one that said I needed to sign up in the competition tent for a baking time, he told me he'd go do that while I waited for Gram and Mimi.

I stood by myself looking at the long list of Fun in the Sun contests listed on the whiteboard. There were competitions for everything from baking, to singing, to dancing, and sewing. The very last contest listed was, "Kooky Karaoke" for ensemble groups doing *fun* karaoke.

It was the only karaoke performance contest listed that didn't require a qualifying round. I guess the point of a kooky performance wasn't so much singing talent, but instead just pure entertainment value. It was too bad that Gram wasn't part of some goofy group. At least then, she'd have a chance to sing.

When Brandon, Gram, and Mimi came back, we all decided to head across the fairgrounds to see what kind of rides there were, but, before we walked away from the whiteboard, I saw

Brandon grab another list of contest rules from one of the envelopes hanging at the edge of the whiteboard. As we walked toward the rides, I wondered if Brandon was planning to enter a contest himself. It gave me a whole new sick feeling in my stomach, because I was sure if <u>he</u> entered something, he'd win. And I knew I couldn't compete with those odds no matter how good my cookies were.

LOVE,
ME

DEAR ME,

Much later that afternoon we checked in to the Borlandsville Fairground Hotel, and not long after that, Mom called me. Thankfully I was down in the hotel lobby by myself getting some ice when my phone rang, because as soon as I heard her voice, even though Dad really had convinced me that Mom was okay, I blubbered like a baby.

Mom was probably the only one who could make me cry so hard and so fast. But that also meant she was the only one who could make me stop, and I finally stopped long enough to have an actual conversation with her.

The bad part about that was that Mom's first question was one I didn't think I should answer.

She wanted to know how Gram's karaoke contests were going. I couldn't very well tell her about all that right now. If I did, she was likely to have another anxiety attack of legendary proportion, and the thought of that made me feel like I might have one too.

So, my answer was, "It's a long story."

And then I added, "It'll be better if I tell you about it in person."

That's when Mom told me that I might get to tell her in person much quicker than we thought. Dad was checking flights to see if she could fly down and meet up with us at the Borlandsville Fair. That way, Mom could drive back to Sunny Sandy Shores with us.

I objected, not because I didn't want to see Mom. I really did! But I worried that traveling might cause Mom more stress.

"Shouldn't you just stay home and rest?"

Mom told me that the doctor said there was no reason she couldn't travel. In fact, he had told her that it would be a great idea for her to get away.

"But what about work?" I asked. "Did you finish what you went home for?"

"Well, here's the thing..."

Mom stopped talking and was quiet for a few seconds and then she said, "I really wanted to wait until we were to together to tell you this, but..."

All I could think was,

OH.
MY.
GOSH!

It hadn't just been anxiety after all.

Mom was going to tell me she was dying of something.

I wondered what an anxiety attack felt like, because now I was sure I was having one.

"I'm likely going to lose my job."

"WHAT?!"

That was not what I expected Mom to say.

Lose her job?!

How could that be?!

Mom was the queen of Make It, Take It.

So, while my head felt like it was spinning faster than the Cyclone ride at the Borlandsville Fair, Mom told me about how lately the executives weren't really "in love" with her new ideas. They just didn't think she was on the "cutting edge of creativity in the twenty-first century."

Hearing this made me mad.

Not creative?!

Mom was the most creative person in the world!

And her ideas?!

They were always the epitome of inspired.

Mom said she just kept thinking that if she worked harder, she'd be able to convince the higher-ups that her ideas were

still relevant. She had been hopeful that her Dear Me Journal would be the turning point. That's why she'd been putting so much time into the project. But she said all her hard work hadn't convinced anybody of anything.

In the end, the executives said they just didn't see the Dear Me Journal as a "viable way to record memories." And they "killed" the project.

Are you thinking what I'm thinking?

Not a viable way to record memories?!

What a bunch of numskulls!

Clueless and nuts is how I'd describe them.

They probably wouldn't know a good memory if it took them by the lapels of their fancy suits and stared them in the face.

The Dear Me Journal Mom had given me had not only been a "viable way to record memories," but it had been my lifeboat in the middle of a shipwreck in the middle of a hurricane.

Mom went on to tell me that when the executives killed her project, she fell apart.

And after her little "breakdown," that's what Mom called it, she said she realized that she had been missing out on so many things in life, including being down in Florida with Gram and me, all for a product that was never even going to see the light of day.

She said it made her sick to think that she had spent her whole career at Make It, Take It helping other people preserve their memories, while forfeiting so many of her own.

When she said that last part, she sounded like she might cry.

So, I have to admit that after hearing the details of Mom's breakdown—even though I felt really bad about what she was going through—I felt somewhat elated to hear that my bratty sarcasm wasn't the cause of Mom's anxiety.

(Even so, I knew after all this, I'd be toning down my rancor a little. Actually, maybe more than a little.)

You might be thinking that I should've jumped right in and told her all about these letters I'm writing and about how it was going to be such a great way to cherish the memories I'd made with Gram.

But Mom had just told me that Make It, Take It was why she ended up in the hospital. Even if the executives changed their minds about Mom's project this time, what would happen when Mom needed to come up with her next idea for a new product?

Would she end up with another anxiety attack, or worse yet, maybe a heart attack this time?

And the even bigger question was, did I really want to try to save Mom's job at Make It, Take It when she had just told me that her job had stolen so many of her chances to make some of her own memories with me?

Maybe because you're older and a lot smarter, you think the answers to these questions seem obvious. But they're not obvious to me. I'm not at all sure what I'm supposed to do. So right now, more than ever, I wish you could write to me, because I'd love to know what you would do if you were me right now.

LOVE,
ME

DEAR ME,

After my phone call with Mom, I headed back to the hotel room. As I walked down the hallway, I thought about the pros and cons of telling Mom about my Dear Me Journal, but that whole dilemma flew out of my mind the minute I walked into the room where we were staying.

Here's why:

Mimi sat on the footstool, which she had pushed up against the bed. She held two wooden spoons in her hands, and she looked like she was pretending they were drumsticks and that the bed was a drum. Gram stood next to her holding a broom like it was a guitar, and Brandon stood in between them with my hairbrush up to his mouth like it was a microphone.

↑
Drumsticks,
apparently

"I signed us up for the Kooky Karaoke Contest!" Brandon said like I should've been as excited as that gas station guy must've been when he realized he won the lottery.

I have to tell you that at this point, if it was possible for a

person's brain to short-circuit, mine would've sent sparks shooting out of my ears followed by plumes of smoke coming out of every one of my hair follicles.

It's not as if when I'd seen the Kooky Karaoke Contest listed on the competition board at the fair that it hadn't crossed my mind that it could've been a chance for Gram to sing karaoke, but that fleeting thought did not include me being part of that ensemble. (Or Mimi and Brandon, for that matter.)

I stood speechless staring at the three of them, while they all jumped in to explain.

Mimi praised "Brandy" for finding a way for Gram to get to sing karaoke after all.

Brandon boasted that besides having the "stupendously wonderful" plan to sign "us" up for the contest, he'd had the idea of calling hotel housekeeping to get the props they were using for their "pretend" instruments.

(I probably don't have to tell you that "stupendously wonderful" were my words, not Brandon's. And even though I also probably don't have to tell you that my sarcasm here was off the charts, I feel compelled to do so, because I don't want you to miss a single nuance of the situation.)

Brandon chattered on and said, "We reshaped a wire hanger

that we found in the closet to look like a tambourine. That'll be perfect for you, Sam!"

Gram explained that Brandon was going to sing lead, and she, Mildred, and I would sing backup.

Gram finished by saying, "That way I'll get to sing, but won't have to be a nervous wreck like I was at 3XB. Who knows if I ever could've even pulled off singing by myself anyway? That's what makes Brandon's idea so brilliant!"

"What a way to save the trip!" Mimi said.

And I know, that you know, exactly what I was thinking when Gram said that Brandon was brilliant and Mimi said he had just saved the trip.

But again, I'm feeling compelled to put it down on paper.

Brilliant?!

Really?!

And saving the trip?!

Are we really going to go through that again?

What about all my ideas?

What about all I'd done?

I'd like to think that if it weren't for me, we'd still be sitting in Gram's Mustang in a muddy ditch at the side of the swamp.

Or we might've had to build a raft to escape the flash floods.

Or perhaps worst of all, our bladders would've burst if I hadn't rallied the troops with the courage necessary to venture into that detestable gas station restroom.

But apparently everyone was suffering from short-term memory loss.

I was so overwhelmed by scorn for Brandon getting so much credit, but at the same time, I was also overwhelmed by an insurmountable question.

Get up in front of the entire Borlandsville Fun in the Sun County Fair crowd and do kooky karaoke?

Were these people bonkers?

Which is exactly the question that came out of my mouth.

"Have you guys gone completely bonkers?"

"What? It'll be fun!" Brandon said. "We're going to sing 'Last Train to Clarksville' by The Monkees. Do you know that song?"

Brandon didn't even wait for me to answer.

He was too excited about us making fools of ourselves. He explained how his brother Duncan was in a band, and they played "Last Train to Clarksville" all the time. And it's one of his favorite songs. And blah, blah, blah.

The honest truth was that Mimi, Gram, and Brandon all seemed like they'd <u>missed</u> the last train to Clarksville.

It seemed like they'd gotten on the <u>first</u> train to Loonytown by mistake.

Or maybe on purpose.

I wasn't really sure.

I stood staring at the three of them wishing there really <u>were</u> a last train to Clarksville, because if there were, I'd buy a ticket and get on it to get away from all this.

"C'mon, Sam," Gram said. "It'll be fun!"

And before I even had time to think of something to say, Brandon shoved the wire-hanger tambourine at me. Then he swiped his phone screen and tapped, and the intro music played.

Gram and Mimi pretended to jam on their "instruments," and Brandon swayed back and forth with my hairbrush pressed up against his chin. I stood with a tight, tense death grip on the wire hanger, paralyzed by the ungainliness of the entire scene.

And to think that on my first day in Florida I'd been embarrassed by Gram's prescription driving glasses and her leopard-print babushka scarf.

That was nothing!

I couldn't figure out why someone as cool as Brandon didn't

my "instrument"

see the cringeworthiness of all this. But when Brandon began to sing, I realized why Brandon was so excited.

He was actually a really good singer.

I'd heard him singing during the car sing-along way back on day one of our trip, but that had been with Gram and Mimi's warbling voices in the background. Singing the first verse by himself, a song he'd obviously sung before, his voice sounded amazing.

That was going to make this whole thing even worse!

Forget about brilliant ideas and saving the say, he'd be a star.

He was going to be the undiscovered talent in the Kooky Karaoke Contest, which meant I was going to look even more magnificently pathetic.

They'd probably bring the Borlandsville County news crew out to do an interview with Brandon after our performance, and he'd be on the five o'clock news.

Gram, Mimi, and I would be on some viral video with the tag, "Borlandsville Backup Singers Cause Fair-goers to Back WAY Up (Preferably out of Earshot)."

I could tell by the way Gram strummed her broom and the way Mimi pounded on the bed with her wooden spoon drumsticks that they didn't care what they looked like. And when

229

they joined Brandon on the chorus, it was painfully obvious that they didn't care what they sounded like either. But I _did_ care, and as I ruminated over what the crowd would think when the four of us got up onstage together, my stomach flip-flopped like I was riding the Zipper, the scariest-looking ride at the fair.

LOVE,
ME

DEAR ME,

The next morning just before my scheduled baking time, Gram and Mimi dropped Brandon and me at the fairground entrance. Gram said she was tired because she hadn't slept well, so she and Mimi went back to the hotel, so she could rest.

I hoped Gram was telling the truth and that she really was just tired, but I couldn't help wondering if something else could be wrong.

I'd checked her pill container the night before to make sure she'd taken her medicine, and she had.

But what if the urgent care doctor was mistaken and there really <u>was</u> something wrong with Gram?

I never thought <u>Mom</u> would've ended up in the hospital, but, completely out of the blue, she had. So even with that all-clear from the urgent care center, part of me was still anxious about Gram's health.

But with chocolate chip cookies to bake, wire tambourines to play, and me still feeling slighted because of Brandon getting the credit for <u>everything</u>, I didn't have much brain space left to fret about Gram.

Brandon helped me carry my ingredients to the competition

231

tent. He could only carry one shopping bag because of his wrist, but I was still thankful for his help, because the bags of baking supplies we'd bought at a nearby grocery store earlier that morning were heavy, and the walk was long.

But I was also grateful because I knew I didn't really deserve his help. Ever since he'd signed us up for that karaoke contest, causing Gram and Mimi to act like he was king of this road trip, I'd been pretty quiet and cold to him.

I knew I wasn't being fair, but that wasn't enough to inspire me to turn things around and be grateful.

Brandon was clearly oblivious to how I was feeling about everything, because he talked incessantly about how excited he was about our performance the next day.

He couldn't wait to tell Duncan.

He couldn't wait to see the look on the audience's faces.

He couldn't wait to see if our act won a prize.

It was pretty amazing since the only thing I couldn't wait for was for it to be over.

At my assigned baking station, Brandon reminded me that the rules said I could have someone help me until I actually started making my cookies, so he asked if I wanted some help setting up.

All I could think was that if I didn't watch out, Brandon might take credit for my cookies just because he helped by carrying <u>one</u> grocery bag to my station.

I told him I didn't need any help.

But then he told me he really <u>wanted</u> to help.

"Maybe while I help you set up, you could tell me how you make your chocolate chip cookies so I can try making them at home."

Wasn't it enough that he was a baseball superstar and an awesomely talented singer, not to mention pretty much cuter than any of the boys at my entire middle school?

Again, I knew I was being a super slug and the sarcasm my inner voice was using to have a conversation with myself in my head skyrocketed so high that it wasn't even in this galaxy anymore. But sometimes, even when you know you're being unreservedly impossible, it's hard to give up your unreasonableness. Mine was gritting its teeth and digging in its heels.

And I guess because of that, my sneering scorn leaked out,

233

and I said, "You know what, Brandon, I wouldn't want you to hurt your wrist."

I don't know who was more surprised by what I said and how I said it.

Me.

Or Brandon.

He wanted to know what <u>that</u> was supposed to mean, and when I looked at him and those "adorable" eyes looked back at me, all my frustrations came to the surface.

"Don't act like you don't know what it means!" I said with way too much disdain in my voice, even for me.

Then I unloaded on him like a dump truck dropping a truck-load of that swampy mud that had splashed up in our faces way back on the first day of the road trip.

"I'm sick of you getting all kinds of credit any time you do anything even remotely helpful.

"Especially when in every single crisis, all you ever do is hold up your phone trying to get cell service.

"And it's so plain to see that you're milking that wrist injury just so you can get out of the gargantuan, Herculean stuff you keep <u>pretending</u> you <u>wish</u> you could do that would actually help."

The fact that I used the words "gargantuan" and "Herculean"

when talking to a fellow middle schooler only proves just how crazed I was.

I was definitely not in my right mind, which was why I kept going.

I told him I couldn't believe he was getting so much glory just for signing us all up for that idiotic karaoke contest.

I told him he didn't care about how laughable I was going to look, because he knew he was going to be the star. As usual.

Then I told him it was pretty apparent to me that he didn't think I was cool, but I knew he didn't care because I also knew he thought he was outrageously cool.

When I said the part about him thinking he was outrageously cool, I heard that ringing in my ears, you know that sound you hear super loud in your head when you get caught red-handed for something. Or when you realize someone probably knows you just stretched the truth so far that it snapped like a taut rubber band.

The ringing clanged in my head, because deep down I knew Brandon had never really acted like he thought of himself as cool. I was the one who thought of him as cool.

If I was honest, I had to admit, that he hadn't ever really done one single thing to make a case for what I'd just said.

But having that truth fill up my head only made me feel more atrocious.

Then Brandon did the worst thing he could do.

He turned and walked away.

WITHOUT SAYING ANYTHING.

And a tear dripped onto the counter of my workstation.

Thankfully the competition tent was noisy with all the other bakers focused on their recipes, so no one had paid any attention to the bratty girl who had just made a gargantuan and Herculean scene.

I'd used baking as therapy innumerable times, but I'd never cried while I baked. Yet there in the Borlandsville Fun in the Sun competition tent, I had to use innumerable paper towels to dry off the counter before I could even begin measuring out the flour and sugar.

Good thing baking was the best therapy, because if I ever needed therapy it was right then.

I was grateful I'd made my chocolate chip cookies so many times that I could do it on autopilot. I could go through the

motions of making them without even having to think about it. That way, while the mixer whirred to combine the ingredients, transforming them into sticky dough, I thought about how much stickier the mess was that I'd made for myself with Brandon by spewing my venom all over him.

And what I realized by the time I was dropping blobs of dough onto my baking sheet was that I'd spent my entire school year, the beginning of this summer, and much of this road trip feeling sorry for myself. All that self-pity piled up inside me until I reached my tipping point, and then I'd dumped it all over Brandon, because he happened to be the one standing nearby.

I knew what I had to do, so I finished baking my cookies, put them in the competition container at my station, and ran them over to the judges' table.

I grabbed my backpack, which luckily had my Dear Me Journal in it, and headed to an empty bench in the corner of the competition tent. I sat down and wrote this letter, hoping it would help me sort out what I needed to sort out in order to maybe fix things with Brandon.

And now that I'm finished reminding you what a sometimes-horrible person you were when you were twelve, I'm headed to the picnic area. It's where Gram and Mimi are supposed to meet

237

Brandon and me later. I hope I can find Brandon before Gram and Mimi get there, and if I can, I hope I have the guts to be <u>un</u>-horrible and give him the most sincere apology ever.

Even though we're not wearing our bowling shirts anymore since we both got those new clothes at Stretch Your Dollar, I really hope Brandon will forgive me so that we can go back to being Team Road Trip again.

I'll write again soon to let you know if it's a win or a loss.

LOVE,
ME

P.S. I wouldn't say this to anyone except you, but in my consternation and distress over what I said to Brandon, my subconscious must've been super focused on making my cookies. As a result, I may have just baked my most outstanding batch of chocolate chip cookies ever. And you're the only one I would admit this to, but I'm secretly hoping they might just be good enough to win some kind of an award.

DEAR ME,

When I saw Brandon in the far corner of the fairground picnic area, Mimi's new plastic purse tablecloth was spread out in front of him. As predicted, her other tablecloth had been left behind at the 3XB, but not just because it would never have been deemed clean enough to use again after covering one of those backyard beach bar picnic tables. It was also because Gram had left in an ambulance, and folding up the tablecloth to take it with us wasn't a super high priority.

Mimi had bought another tablecloth when we shopped for stuff to make my cookies. And though she liked that it was Florida-themed with palm trees and coconuts printed on it, she said it was practically a sin to pay grocery-store prices for the same thing she could've gotten at the Treasures for Pennies store she always shopped at back at Sunny Sandy Shores. But she also said, no matter what the cost, she didn't see how we could get by without a new tablecloth, especially while we were traveling.

Since the new tablecloth was there, I knew Gram and Mimi had already come back to the fair, but I didn't see them.

As I headed toward Brandon, my stomach felt as nauseous as if I'd eaten all my cookie dough instead of baking it, but I knew the longer I waited to face Brandon, the harder it would be to apologize. I also knew I might only have a few minutes before Gram and Mimi came back from wherever it was that they were, and it was bad enough that Brandon knew how horrible I could be. I didn't need Gram and Mimi knowing too.

As soon as Brandon saw me coming, that ball-of-cookie-dough feeling in my stomach traveled up my esophagus and turned into a boulder of pure panic in the middle of my chest.

And I wondered if anxiety attacks were hereditary.

I wasn't exactly sure how to apologize to Brandon. Except for arguments with my sisters, I'd never really unloaded on someone like I'd done with him.

With Tori and Annalise, it was usually Mom or Dad who sort of forced us to apologize to each other.

But apologizing to Brandon was completely different.

For one thing, he hadn't done anything to deserve my wrath, and that was never true with my sisters. Even when I was completely in the wrong, they were usually somehow at least a little bit to blame.

But the bigger difference was...it was Brandon.

Brandon.

I really wasn't sure that I could keep myself from throwing up.

But before I knew it, I was standing right in front of him.

We both said, "Hey," in quiet voices as the fairground crowds talked, laughed, and ate all around us.

Then something really, surprising happened.

When I opened my mouth to start my apology by saying, "I'm sorry," Brandon said the same thing first.

What?!

What was he sorry about?

On the walk across the picnic area to where Brandon was, I'd been thinking about what I wanted to say, but now that he said he was sorry, I'd forgotten everything I'd rehearsed in my head.

"What in the world are you sorry about?"

He said, "You were right about a lot of stuff."

I couldn't figure out what he was talking about, because I didn't really think I was right about anything. So, I didn't know what to say.

But it was obvious that Brandon had also rehearsed what he wanted to say, because he kept talking.

He told me that he could totally see why I was mad at him for stealing the glory for saving the trip. He said Duncan did stuff like that all the time at home, and it really bugged him.

Hearing that made me realize that, even though Brandon's

241

good looks were what I had noticed about him right away, his niceness was even more attractive.

The only bad part about that was that it made me feel even more unattractive because of how un-nice I'd been to him.

Next Brandon said that he had kind of been a "baby" about his wrist, but his injury was sort of complicated.

I wasn't sure what that meant, but I didn't have time to think about it because the next thing Brandon said was that, even though I had been right about some stuff, there were two things that I'd been really wrong about.

"I guess you're entitled to your opinion, but, just so you know, I don't really think of myself as all that cool."

I couldn't help but think of what a cool thing that was to say.

But then the second thing he said that I'd gotten all wrong was even "cooler."

"If you're entitled to your opinion. I'm entitled to mine, and I think you're pretty cool."

Brandon thought I was cool?!

But he didn't stop there.

He also told me he thought I was brave for suggesting we get out of Gram's Mustang just after seeing that alligator so that we could try to push the car.

"I was scared to death that alligator would come back, but it didn't seem to bother you at all. And then you climbed through the window at Glory Bound Baptist like you were a cat burglar or something," he joked. "You were just never afraid to do whatever we needed you to do."

It was hard to get my head around everything Brandon was saying, but even if my head couldn't understand it, my heart could. And as a result, it floated like one of the fairground helium balloons that lined the edges of the game booths.

"This trip has been such a blast," Brandon said. "We've probably had more fun in a few days than most kids will end up having all summer."

And then, as if that wasn't remarkable enough, something really, awesome happened.

"And just so you know I really mean it. Here."

Brandon reached down to the picnic bench he was sitting on and handed me a white ribbon that said, "Road Trip MVP" in gold glitter.

He had made it in the craft booth while I was making my cookies.

Mom always used the expression, "Kill them with kindness," and that was exactly what Brandon had just done.

So, yes, my heart soared, but if I really was the King Kong of super slugs sliming my way across the floor, Brandon had just run over me with a huge semi, flattening me out beyond recognition.

What could I say now that wouldn't sound completely bogus after all that he'd just said to me?

But what choice did I have?

First, I said, "Thanks," for the ribbon. Then I sat down across from him at the picnic table. I told him how sorry I was for everything that I'd said.

"You didn't deserve to get yelled at, and the truth is everything I said had way more to do with me than you."

Then, probably because he had told me things about himself that I wasn't expecting to hear, I told him things about myself that I wasn't expecting to say.

I told him about my year of sixth grade and all its disappointments.

I told him that my chocolate chip cookies were so good only because I'd had so much practice making them because of all my failures.

And I told him that I hadn't even wanted to come to Florida to visit Gram this summer.

He listened but didn't say anything.

"When I heard about this road trip, I dreaded it like the plague," I swallowed hard and added, "especially when I found out you were coming along."

Once I said that last part, we both laughed, and we laughed even harder when I told him I had thought he was a girl.

But then I told him the trip had been tons of fun for me, too, and I couldn't imagine what it would've been like without him.

I couldn't believe I had actually said all that.

Out loud.

To a boy.

Especially a boy like Brandon.

After I finished talking, Brandon was quiet for a few seconds, and I worried that because of everything we'd said to each other, things were going to be awkward between us, but then Brandon said, "I have a confession to make."

Brandon sounded super serious, and my cookie dough stomachache came back again in an instant.

"I ended up on this road trip because I lied."

"Lied?!" I said. "About what?"

"The reason why I said my wrist injury is complicated is because my wrist isn't really injured anymore. I'm just pretending it is because of baseball."

"What? Why?"

"I'm kinda sick of baseball. I mean, I don't hate it, but... I don't know, I started playing because Duncan played. And I liked it in the beginning, but once I started pitching, and people thought I was good, there was so much pressure. I played on my school team and made all-conference. Then got recruited to play for the park district team, and when I got MVP, my dad signed me up for a traveling team. Before I knew it, all I ever did was play baseball. I never had time to do anything else."

It was hard for me to process everything Brandon was saying, and part of me felt myself getting a little bit annoyed with Brandon again.

How could a person be so good at something and then not want to do it?

I would've killed to be a superstar at something.

But what Brandon said next quieted that whiny voice of self-pity inside me.

"Last spring when I got hurt, and I couldn't play, I realized how great it was to just hang out with my friends again and do stuff besides play baseball. But the biggest thing I realized was that I really didn't miss baseball all that much. So, when I went back to the doctor to get my splint off, I told the doctor my wrist still hurt, even though it didn't. He told me I should wear the splint for another month.

"That's the only reason I'm still wearing this thing, and it's also the only reason I got to come on this trip."

Brandon had actually needed to lie in order to get to do what he wanted. That really made me feel sad for him.

Then I thought about something that had never occurred to me.

Did I really like all the things that I'd attempted to be good at?

Or had I just wanted to be good at something?

Anything.

I think I always assumed that if you were good at something, you'd automatically like doing it, but from what Brandon just told me, that wasn't necessarily true.

"Why don't you just tell your parents you don't want to play baseball anymore?"

Then Brandon told me that what made it so complicated was Duncan.

Duncan had played baseball when he was younger and had been super talented. After high school, he tried out for the minors but didn't make it.

Duncan was disappointed, but Brandon said his dad was devastated.

So, Duncan decided to go to college and play for a college team in hopes of eventually being able to break into the minors, but at college Duncan discovered something else. Music.

And he loved it.

Duncan and three of his friends formed a band, and now Duncan didn't even want to play baseball anymore. That was why now, Brandon's dad had all his baseball hopes pinned on Brandon.

Because of all that, Brandon didn't see how he could ever tell his dad that he didn't want to play anymore.

"But because of Duncan, I found out how much I love music. I really want to take voice lessons, but I don't think my dad would be too wild about that, especially since he kind of thinks Duncan's wasting his time playing in a band."

My head churned with all this unexpected information, and one of the things that rose to the top was a question I had for Brandon.

"So, as long as we're making confessions here. Tell me the truth. Did you sign us up for the Kooky Karaoke Contest because of Gram or because of you?"

Brandon looked at me with those adorable eyes, and I knew the answer without him even having to say anything, so I didn't make him answer. I just asked him another question.

"Don't you think we're going to make fools of ourselves?"

To which Brandon answered, "Of course."

And then he went on to say that that was the point, and that it would be fun.

"That's easy for you to say. You have a good voice. I don't," I said. "And in case you haven't realized it, Gram and Mimi don't have very good voices either. I just spent all last school year making a fool of myself by getting up in front of people and showcasing my lack of talent. Believe me. It's not that fun!"

"Kooky Karaoke isn't about the talent. I'll bet you a fairground turkey leg that doing the contest with Gram and Mimi will be fun," Brandon said. "If our goal is to be kooky there's no way we won't succeed. And embracing the kooky will definitely be fun."

I laughed but told him that even if I made the bet with him, and the contest somehow did end up being fun, I'd never buy him one of those disgusting turkey legs.

Then I surprised myself, and I think I surprised Brandon too, by saying, "If we do the contest and it actually turns out to be fun, you and I have to ride the Ferris wheel together before we head back to Sunny Sandy Shores."

Brandon held out his hand and said, "Deal!"

And as we shook hands to make the bet official, Gram and Mimi walked up to the picnic table, but neither of them said "Hi," because they both had a mouthful of food.

They each held a huge Borlandsville Fun in the Sun County Fair turkey leg and looked about as happy as a couple fair-going senior citizens could possibly look.

LOVE,
ME

DEAR ME,

While music blasted from the stage speakers, I paced back and forth. I couldn't believe how nervous I was.

Maybe it was because the crowd gathered for the Kooky Karaoke Contest was way past huge.

Maybe it was because the 1960s-style outfits we found at the nearby thrift store we had passed last night on the way back to the hotel from the fair made us look ridiculous.

Or maybe it was just because here I was again about to make a huge fool of myself in public.

I'd already baked cookies yesterday, so what would I do for therapy if this went wrong?

I kept wondering why I'd let Brandon convince me the contest would be fun.

The four of us had laughed a lot while we spent all morning and most of the afternoon practicing the song in the hotel room.

And while Brandon and I had eaten lunch, we had a good time making a huge cardboard cutout of a train that Gram and I planned to sort of chug across the stage during the final chorus of "Last Train to Clarksville."

But as the three high school girls who performed right before our act stomped around on the wooden stage in furry snow boots, pink ballerina tights, and tiny tutus singing "Achy Breaky Heart," I thought my heart might explode with apprehension.

Brandon and Mimi looked nervous too, but not over-the-cliff nervous like me.

Gram, on the other hand looked terrified.

She sat in a folding chair near the backstage steps fanning herself with a fairground flyer. She kept complaining of feeling faint, and she said she had a headache.

But we all just told her she was nervous.

"You're finally going to sing karaoke for a crowd, Madge," Mimi said.

"Yeah, the audience is going to love how you play broomstick air guitar," Brandon said trying to make Gram feel better.

"And just think how good it will feel when it's over," I said, giving myself a pep talk as much as giving Gram one.

Then we heard the crowd begin to clap along with the snow boots ballerina cowgirls, and when we heard the crowd start to sing along too, Brandon said, "C'mon, you guys! We had so much fun practicing. We can't let our nerves ruin it for us now."

I took a deep breath and tried to let go of some of my trepidation.

Brandon was right. There had been more than a few times while we rehearsed in the hotel room that the four of us laughed so uncontrollably that we doubled over and couldn't even talk, let alone sing.

Mimi had gotten so "into" drumming that during one of our "run-throughs" one of her wooden spoons had slipped out of her hand and gone flying across the hotel room.

Gram had to actually duck so that she didn't get hit in the forehead with the airborne drumstick-spoon.

After one of our "take five" water breaks, which we took often to be sure Gram stayed hydrated, I looked at Brandon and saw a clump of my hair from his microphone-hairbrush stuck to one of the buttons of his thrift-store shirt, which he had unbuttoned almost all the way down to his wide belt so that he looked the part of a lead singer. But the clump of hair made him look like he had a hairy chest and gave him the look of a gorilla instead of the lead singer of a '60s band.

But when my wire hanger tambourine caught the edge of the drapes that I was standing near, causing me to pull down the whole curtain rod, Mimi ran to the bathroom and made it there just before peeing her pants.

I don't know what was funnier. Seeing Mimi run to the bathroom or hearing her tell us she almost "peed her pants."

So yes, Brandon was right, we needed to go out onstage and have as much fun as, or maybe even more fun than, we'd had practicing.

But by the beginning of the last chorus of "Achy Breaky Heart," Gram pulled on my arm to get my attention.

I leaned down and she said, "Sam, I don't think I can do this. I'm really feeling sick."

I rubbed Gram's shoulder and told her again that she was just nervous, but Brandon and Mimi had heard what Gram said.

"Maybe she is sick," Mimi said. "She's been feeling tired since yesterday."

But I told Gram again that it was just nerves, and then I said, "Just think how proud Grandpa would be of you right now."

Gram sighed and said, "I don't know, Sam."

And when the last note of "Achy Breaky Heart" played, the crowd clapped super loud, and Brandon said, "Maybe we shouldn't go on."

"But we have to!" I insisted.

It just couldn't be that we had come all this way, endured so many hardships, and gotten <u>this</u> close, only to give up and walk away now.

Brandon was right. It was going to be fun if we could swallow our nervousness and let the kookiness we'd embraced while singing our hearts out back in the hotel room be unleashed.

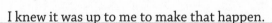

I knew it was up to me to make that happen.

"We have to go on!" I said. "C'mon, Brandon, help me get Gram up."

We both put our hands under Gram's armpits and pulled her out of the folding chair, which was almost as hard as pushing her up that wooden bunk bed ladder back at Camp Wonderful.

While the Achy Breaky cowgirls stomped down the stairs, we grabbed our cardboard train to Clarksville and our "instruments" and climbed the stage steps ourselves.

I heard a quiet little rumble of muffled laughter as we took our places, but I wasn't surprised.

Skinny Mimi wore a short-sleeved sweater vest and a velvet miniskirt with white go-go boots. She stood behind the stool she was going to use as a drum.

Gram was dressed in flowered bell-bottoms and a leather

jacket that we'd found at the last minute in the bottom of the thrift-store clearance bin. She gripped her broomstick guitar, still looking scared but ready to jam.

I was wearing an orange-and-yellow minidress and white tights and held my wire hanger tambourine like it was a real instrument.

And Brandon strutted his stuff wearing his unbuttoned shirt with the superlong pointed collar. With the microphone held up to his mouth, he looked poised for our performance.

I don't know if you've ever seen the television show <u>The Monkees</u> online, but the four of us looked like we could've been guest stars on it.

So, that ripple of laughter before our song even played didn't surprise me.

But thankfully, even though it was still daylight, there were bright stage lights making it impossible to see the fair-goers who gathered to watch us, because if I was going to make it through the performance, I knew I'd have to pretend I was back at the hotel room instead of onstage with all these people staring at us.

My nervous stomach fluttered as we waited for the music. I looked at Gram and Mimi on one side of me and Brandon on the other. For a minute I couldn't quite believe we were actually

going to do this, but then the music started, and the minute I heard Brandon's singing voice come through the stage speakers, reality set in.

It took a line or two of lyrics before Brandon sounded like himself, but when I heard Gram and Mimi start their backup singing, I sang too.

And by the time we got to the chorus.

WE.
WERE.
JAMMING!

The four of us sang and danced and pretended to play.

The audience loved us!

And by the time Gram and I put down our guitar and tambourine, grabbed that cardboard train to Clarksville, and scooted it across the front of the stage, the crowd's applause roared.

We had done it!

Gram had gotten to sing karaoke!

Her widow's bucket list dream had come true!

And though singing karaoke hadn't been my dream, I

realized that standing onstage with the crowd going wild for us was the feeling I had been after all year.

Gram and I put down the train and the four of us walked to the edge of the stage and took a bow.

As I came up from our bow, the crowd gasped, and I felt something land on my left foot.

I looked down.

Gram lay at my feet.

She had collapsed.

Again.

"Gram! Gram!" I yelled over the noise and confusion.

Then I dropped to my knees next to her.

And Brandon yelled, "Call nine-one-one!"

I grabbed Gram's wrist to feel her pulse, and the rhythm of her heart raced like a runaway locomotive. But when I put my ear to her mouth, her breath felt shallow.

No matter how many times I said "Gram," and no matter how many of my tears fell on her face or dripped onto the leather-fringed jacket she wore, she didn't open her eyes.

That was all not even an hour ago, but it feels more like a few hundred years, because I'm sitting in the Borlandsville emergency-room waiting area with Mimi on one side of me

and Brandon on the other. And now that I'm finished writing this letter, I don't know what I'll do to keep myself from going completely hysterical, because since we've gotten here, no one has told us anything at all about what's wrong with Gram or how she's even doing.

I think you'd agree that there's only one worse thing that could happen in this situation, and no matter how ingrained that camp motto is in my head, I don't even want to think about that, let alone prepare for it.

LOVE,
ME

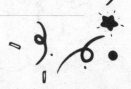

DEAR ME,

I didn't know it at the time, but the emergency-room doctor called Mom shortly after we got here. Mimi must've given them Mom's number when she gave the nurses all Gram's information.

So, a little while ago, Mom called me.

I cried while Mom <u>tried</u> to talk.

And ever since then, I've been sitting in the corner of the emergency-room waiting area writing you another letter.

I won't keep you in suspense.

Gram didn't die.

And the really good news is that Mom said the doctor told her Gram's going to be okay, but I'm not so sure about me, especially because of what Mom told me next.

The doctor told Mom that Gram hadn't been taking her medication.

I exploded with a whole new batch of tears.

"How can that be? Her pill container's been empty."

But Mom had more to say, so she tried to calm me down, so I could listen.

I guess once Gram regained consciousness at the hospital, she confessed

to the doctor that she'd stopped taking her blood pressure and cholesterol medication on purpose. She hadn't taken it since we'd left Sunny Sandy Shores.

She hadn't wanted the medicine's side effects to interfere with our trip, the worst of which for her was that the pills made her have to go to the bathroom much more often than usual. Gram told the doctor she just didn't want to be bothered with that while we traveled.

Can you even believe that?!

No wonder Mom gets so mad at Gram sometimes.

But wait until you hear this.

At the beginning of our road trip, Gram somehow had a hunch that I was checking her pill container, so she threw away each day's pills so that I'd think she'd taken them.

Maybe Mom had been right to want Gram in that condo eight and a half minutes from our house. Because if Gram was going to act like this, Mom really <u>did</u> need to keep a closer eye on her.

As I continued to cry, Mom not only consoled me, but she also apologized for having asked me to keep track of Gram like that in the first place.

"I should've never put you in that position," Mom said.

261

She also said <u>she</u> should have never discouraged Gram from moving to Sunny Sandy Shores if that was really what Gram wanted. Mom agreed that Gram was right about not needing her permission to do the things she wanted to do.

"Ever since we lost Grandpa, I've just felt like Gram needed someone to take care of her, but I should've realized that's <u>her</u> job, not mine," Mom said.

"But hasn't she just proven she needs us to tell her what to do, and she also needs us to make sure she does it?"

"She's got to make her own choices and then be willing to accept whatever consequences come."

So, you might be thinking that, since Gram stopped taking her pills on purpose and intentionally tricked me into thinking she <u>was</u> taking them AND since Mom didn't even think it had been fair of her to ask me to keep track of Gram's medication in the first place, you probably think that I'm off the hook and that this proves none of this really was my fault after all.

But the doctor also told Mom that missing a few days of medication wouldn't have been such a big deal or made such a big difference if Gram hadn't been under so much stress. Her fainting had likely been caused by her anxiety, and not her blood pressure.

So now you're probably thinking that, since all the stress of this road trip was in no way my fault, that this was just more evidence that I really was off the hook.

But the stress that happened right before Gram collapsed was because of us singing in the Kooky Karaoke Contest. And that was my fault.

Right before we went onstage, Gram told me she wasn't just nervous.

She told me she wasn't feeling well.

She told me she didn't want to sing.

But I made her do it anyway.

I literally pulled her out of the chair and dragged her up the stage steps.

When I told Mom all that through lots more tears, she told me something else Gram said to the doctor just after he scolded her for not taking her health more seriously.

And what Gram said might just be the most unbelievable thing I've written so far, which is saying a lot.

"Listen, Dr. Whoever You Are, I realize you've gone to medical school, so you're a lot smarter than I am, but I've just had one of the best weeks of my life and gotten to do something I always dreamed of doing. And I couldn't have done any of that if I'd spent the week searching for public restrooms every five minutes and worrying about all the other side effects that come with taking those darned pills.

"Did I put my health at risk? Maybe. But so be it. It was well beyond worth it, no matter what happens to me."

And then Mom said something that made me feel better than I've felt in a really, long time. Maybe even better than I've ever felt.

"So, Sam, if you're the one who pulled Gram up onstage, you should be proud."

**LOVE,
ME**

P.S. So, even though I was feeling pretty awesome after hearing some of the things Mom told me, that awesome feeling had a tiny pinhole in it. And through that tiny pinhole, there was a slow leak causing some of that awesome feeling to deflate.

There's still one thing that's really nagging at my conscience.

I wish I knew for sure what my <u>real</u> reason for pulling Gram up onstage had been.

Was it for <u>her</u> dream?

Or for mine?

Did I do it so that I'd finally get to know what it felt like to have people clap for me?

I wish I knew the answer to that.

DEAR ME,

It's the middle of the night, and we're back at the Borlandsville Fairground Hotel. The doctors released Gram after she promised to take her medication. No. Matter. What!

According to Mom, according to Gram, even according to the doctor in the emergency room, it wasn't my responsibility to make sure Gram took her pills, but even so, until we get back to Sunny Sandy Shores, I plan to watch Gram put those two little pills on her tongue, drink a full glass of water, and swallow them.

Gram and Mimi are both asleep in bed. And of course, snoring away.

Brandon's in the adjoining room, most likely sleeping, and most definitely looking adorable.

I'm in the bathroom writing to you.

And thinking.

Thinking about what Gram said about dreams being worth it.

Thinking about what Brandon said about the pressure he feels to play baseball.

And thinking about what Mom said about missing out on some of her own memories while helping other people cherish and preserve theirs.

And all this thinking has given me a few great ideas.

I think there's a way this Dear Me Journal, which has meant so much to me on this trip, and hopefully means a lot to you now, could also be a way to mean something for other people too.

I started the summer not wanting Mom to bring my Dear Me Journal into a meeting with her executives, and that hasn't changed. I still would never want her to do that. But my opinion of how meaningful Dear Me letters can be has changed drastically.

When this summer started, I wondered how I would survive my visit to Florida.

And once I got to Sunny Sandy Shores, I wondered how I would survive the road trip with Gram, Mimi, and Brandon.

And once we'd left on the trip, I wondered how in the world I'd survive the pitfalls that challenged us around every curve and corner.

Turns out the answer to my survival was these letters to you.

I don't think I could've survived this trip without them.

I don't think I could've survived the trip without you.

Mom said she was pretty sure she was finished with Make It, Take It, but that doesn't mean she has to be finished with her career in preserving memories. Now that I believed in the

Dear Me Journal as much as she did, maybe even more, maybe Mom and I could team up. With me as a spokesperson for the product, Mom and I could start our own little business and sell Dear Me Journals online. It wouldn't be as stressful as working for Make It, Take It, but Mom would still get to keep pursuing her creative dreams, and the two of us could make some memories of our own.

Besides that, I have an idea of my own that we could add to the Dear Me Journal, so that we wouldn't just have one product to sell online; we'd have two.

LETTERS TO LOVED ONES

Record it today, so your loved ones can cherish it tomorrow.

Letters to Loved Ones are a revolutionary way to record vacation memories.

Don't simply record the stops and scenery along the way.

Don't just post photos online of everything you do, for everyone to see.

Make it more memorable for the ones you love.

Make it a personal memento better than any souvenir.

A keepsake that lasts forever.

Write Letters to Loved Ones to those you travel with.

Letters to Loved Ones

A way to do something unforgettable for the loved ones who joined you in creating once-in-a-lifetime memories, you'll never want to forget.

Doing something like this with Mom meant that I'd be way too busy to waste my time in seventh grade trying out for more stuff that probably wouldn't end up being my thing and might not even be all that fun anyway.

It was true that standing on that fairground stage soaking up all that praise felt great, but in all honesty, hearing that Gram had had such a good time on the road trip, knowing that I had played some part in making that happen, and having Mom tell me I should feel proud felt even better.

I hope you don't mind, but on the next several pages of my Dear Me Journal, I'll be writing a few letters and tearing them out so that I can give them to my traveling companions.

But before I give them to their recipients, when Mom gets to Florida, I'll show them to her so that she can get excited about Letters to Loved Ones too. That way, when the two of us get back home, we can take the preserving memories world by storm; and while we do, we'll create some of our own unforgettable memories.

LOVE,
ME

DEAR MIMI,

When I think back to the day I met you, I have to admit, I never would've imagined that just a week later, I'd think of you as my friend. But I do. And I'm lucky. Or as I know you would say, I'm "blessed."

When you called me *precious*, when I found out about your boxes of Bibles, when I realized we would be going on a road trip together, I won't lie and say that I was thrilled. Actually, I was filled with overwhelming dread. But now that our trip is almost over, I hope I never forget the memories that, little by little, replaced my apprehension as we overcame all the "trials" (as you call them) that we had to navigate with sweat and mud, tears, and laughter. Hopefully this letter will help you cherish the moments of this trip long after we return to Sunny Sandy Shores, and I hope the trip will always be something you count as a real blessing. I know I always will.

LOVE,
SAM

P.S. So many things will always make me think of you—things like turtles, hymns like "Marching to Zion," and definitely plastic tablecloths and vanilla-scented hand sanitizer.

DEAR BRANDON,

You already know when I heard you were going on this trip that I wasn't all that happy about it, and you also already know all the pretty jerky things I thought about you before I bothered to get to know you.

But this letter isn't about any of that.

It's about how lucky I am that you came along on this trip.

And how thankful I am that we became friends.

And most of all, it's about how I hope you'll remember all the fun and funny and horrible and horrendous things that happened to the four of us along the way. Those are the things that make the memories from this trip something I want to remember and cherish forever.

(I can't believe I just wrote the word "cherish" in a letter to you. I hope you don't think that's corny.)

So, when we both get old, and don't remember things the way we wish we did, here's a list of things that might help you remember this trip in all its triumph and tragedy:

* Television-theme-song car sing-alongs
* Turtles

* Alligators

* Swamp mud

* Glory Bound Baptist (and the cat burglar)

* Church donation bin outfits

* Team Road Trip shirts

* Camp Wonderful

* Bunk beds (and pushing Gram's butt up the ladder of one)

* Friendly Fill-Up gas station (and the Restroom of Horror)

* 3XB (minus the barbecue)

* Kooky Karaoke Contest ("Last Train to Clarksville")

* A friend named Sam

TEAM ROAD TRIP ROCKS FOREVER,
SAM

P.S. I'm glad you told me the truth about your wrist and about baseball. I hope when you get home, you'll tell that truth to the people who really need to know. I have a feeling, even if they aren't happy about it right away, they will be eventually. Sometimes people's minds have a way of drastically changing even when we think there's no chance they will.

273

DEAR GRAM,

I didn't believe Mom when she told me this trip to visit you would be the "trip of a lifetime." I'm not sure I've ever been so wrong about something.

There's no way to put into words what this trip means to me right now and what I think it will mean to me for the rest of my life.

I hadn't really wanted to come to Florida this summer. Not because I didn't want to see you, but because I wasn't all that excited about spending time at what I thought was going to be a senior citizens' center. And when I found out about the road trip with Mimi and Brandon, I wondered how I'd survive.

But somewhere along the way, I'm not even sure when, the ups and downs of the trip started to change me. The time I was getting to spend with you and the arduous obstacles the four of us kept having to face as we chased your karaoke dream gave me experiences that I know I never want to forget.

And when I heard you agree with Mimi in the urgent care center waiting room that the two of you were having the time of your lives with Brandon and me, I thought my heart might explode with a feeling I don't think I've ever had before.

Then Mom told me what you said to the doctor about it all being worth it, even with your two horrible health scares, and my exploding heart melted like a fireworks finale against a nighttime summer sky. And I knew right then, that even if I'm lucky enough to live to be as old as you, it will be hard for me to have a week as memorable and meaningful as this one.

So, thank you, Gram, for giving me a week's worth of memories to cherish for a lifetime.

LOVE,
SAM

DEAR MOM,

You weren't on the weeklong karaoke Bible-delivery widow's bucket list road trip, but you're the reason I was.

I'm not only thankful to have had a week chock-full of cherish-worthy memories, but I'm thankful that your Dear Me Journal was there to see me through the toughest times of this trip.

Besides that, now that my Dear Me letters are written, I'll get to enjoy this whole trip again and again and again, whenever I want. And I'll get to do that all because of you!

You said that you regret having missed making some of your own memories in exchange for creating projects for other people to preserve theirs. But I'm thankful you're the kind of person who thinks so much of making memories, because now I'm that kind of person too.

I'm glad you figured out you want to spend more time making some of your own memories with me, because I'm looking forward to having fun making them with you.

LOVE,
SAM

DEAR ME,

The next day at the fair, Gram and Mimi sat in the shade in the picnic area with plenty of food spread out on <u>Mimi's tablecloth</u>. They were going to enjoy more of their fairground favorites while Brandon and I hit the rides.

As soon as Brandon and I filled ourselves with all the carnival thrills we could handle, the four of us planned to head to the airport, pick up Mom, and then work our way back to Sunny Sandy Shores.

Lying next to the funnel cakes, cotton candy, and caramel apples on the picnic table were two Borlandsville Fun in the Sun County Fair prize ribbons.

One for an honorable mention in the Kooky Karaoke Contest.

And one for third place in the Baking Competition.

My cookies had actually earned a ribbon, and not just an obligatory participation one!

The prizes had been awarded earlier that morning in the competition tent, and though Gram clapped loud when they announced our karaoke honorable mention, she clapped exponentially louder when they announced my third-place baking prize. Ever since then, she hasn't stopped telling me how proud of me she is.

All of this feels pretty great, but there's something that's making me feel <u>AMAZING</u> and that's the letters I've written to Gram, Mimi, Brandon, and Mom. I can't wait to give them to them when we get back to Sunny Sandy Shores.

It will be the perfect way to end this road trip!

Before Brandon and I headed off toward the rides, Gram said she wished she could be young again.

"I'd give anything to take a turn on the Zipper. I used to love that one!"

"Don't even think about, Madge!" Mimi said.

Then Mimi told us she'd keep an eye on Gram while we were gone, and Gram sort of huffed a little.

Ever since Gram had been released from the emergency room, all three of us had been hovering over her, probably a little too closely. I think it was starting to make her a little nuts.

Mimi told us that she and Gram had a couple of phone calls to make anyway, so between the food they planned to feast on and the people they needed to get in touch with, they had plenty to do.

"Madge needs to call Gert back," Mimi said.

"Gert?!" I said. "Why would you call her?"

"Oh, I guess she's changed her tune a little about my 'quack' of a dermatologist,'" Gram said. "She left me a message saying my doctor saved her life, because one of the skin samples he took at her appointment turned out to be cancer. She called me to thank me. Can you believe it?"

Gram said she was surprised that Gert had stayed in the doctor's office long enough to even have a skin sample taken.

"Only reason she called me back is to alleviate her guilt for the way she acted. I should teach her a lesson by <u>not</u> calling her back."

"Madge," Mimi scolded. "Be the bigger person."

Gram huffed some more, so Mimi changed the subject.

She told us she was going to give Harold a call, just to check in with him to see how his toe was doing as well as to let him know they'd be home later tonight or sometime tomorrow.

"I'm sure he'll be waiting with bated breath," Gram said smirking and raising her eyebrows. "Just tell him we don't want any more of those darned directions."

To which Mimi said, "Madge, really!"

And it occurred to me for the first time that Mimi and toe-fungus, driving-directions Harold might actually *like* each other.

I didn't know whether that was cringey or cute.

So, as Gram and Mimi dug their phones out of their purses, Brandon and I headed over to the carnival rides, and we

HAD
A
BLAST!

We rode the Zipper and the Tilt-a-Whirl.

We drove go-carts and played carnival games.

We jumped in the bounce house and raced down the inflatable slides.

And when we had done it all, I wished we could start over and do it all again, but it was almost time to go to the airport to pick up Mom.

"Well, the only thing left is for us to settle our bet," Brandon said, and we both looked at each other and smiled.

"To the Ferris wheel!" Brandon said as he put his hand up in the air and pointed in that direction.

And as we stood in line, sharing the box of Lemonheads we'd won playing Skee-Ball, I felt about as awesome as a person can feel.

We were both wearing our Team Road Trip shirts. Mimi had

washed them out in the bathroom sink for us the night before. She thought we should wear them on our last day of the trip, and she was right.

And just like the secondhand-store bowling shirts were the perfect thing to wear on the last day of our trip, the Ferris wheel was the perfect way to end our time at the Borlandsville Fun in the Sun County Fair and conclude this out-of-control, widow's bucket list karaoke Bible-delivery road trip.

As I enjoyed the view while the Ferris wheel circled, I thought about how funny it was that it took a trip like the one we'd just been on to:

Have the chocolate chip cookies that came from all my failures win a prize.

Discover something Mom and I can do together that we can both feel proud of.

Find out how cool my grandma really is.

And the bonus part of the trip was meeting someone like Brandon and realizing that the people I so quickly label as "just a little too cool" can actually make pretty great friends.

Now, I don't know if you're thinking this or not. But I sort of wonder, that at this point, in this collection of letters, because this is the last one, and I've set you up with this really sentimental ride on the Ferris wheel, that you might be thinking that I'm going to finish with sort of a semi-surprising bang.

(And no, I don't mean that you're thinking something really bad happened, like the Ferris wheel malfunctioned, and Brandon and I got stuck at the top for hours and hours or maybe even days and days. Although with all the things that have happened to us so far, I guess something like that would not necessarily be out of the question.)

But that's not the kind of thing I'm talking about.

I'm wondering if it hasn't crossed your mind that possibly, at some point during the Ferris wheel ride, that Brandon and I may have become <u>more</u> than just friends.

Maybe you're wondering if Brandon and I held hands.

And in all these letters, I've always written nothing but the truth, and never kept anything from you.

But this is where I have to stop.

Because here's the thing.

If Brandon and I <u>did</u> hold hands, I'm pretty sure you'd remember it.

And if we <u>didn't</u>, maybe you'd rather remember it like we did.

But either way, it doesn't matter, because when I hit the road this summer, what turned out to be important was the ride itself.

The ride Brandon and I took on the Ferris wheel.

And the ride the four of us took together in Gram's Mustang, down so many rural back roads of Florida, doing all the things we'd set out to do and a whole lot more than we could've ever expected or imagined.

That's how each of us ended up with memories that will last a lifetime.

And for me, those memories pretty much changed everything.

LOVE,
ME

CHOCOLATE CHIP COOKIES

* 1 cup granulated sugar
* ½ cup light brown sugar, packed
* 2 eggs
* 1 cup unsalted butter, room temperature
* 1 teaspoon vanilla
* 2¼ cups all-purpose flour
* 1 teaspoon baking soda
* ½ teaspoon salt
* 2 cups semisweet chocolate chips

Optional ingredients to put a Samantha twist on your chocolate chip cookies (use one or all!):

* ½ teaspoon cinnamon
* ½ teaspoon ginger
* ½ teaspoon nutmeg

1. In a large mixing bowl, whisk together sugars, eggs, butter, and vanilla (and the optional ingredients if you choose to include them).

2. Stir in flour, baking soda, salt, and chocolate chips.

3. When ingredients are thoroughly combined, cover bowl and place in a refrigerator for 2 hours to chill.

4. After 2 hours, preheat oven to 375°F.

5. Use tablespoon to drop rounded balls of dough on ungreased cookie sheets. The balls of dough should be 2 to 2½ inches apart.

6. Bake 8 to 10 minutes or until cookies are golden brown.

7. Take cookies out of oven, and place on a wire rack to cool.

A special thanks to my neighbor, Martha, who not only shared more than a few batches of her chocolate chip cookies with my family but also told me the above ingredients were the reason her cookies were so uniquely good. —Nancy J. Cavanaugh

ACKNOWLEDGMENTS

After finishing a book, it's always difficult to know who to thank first. This time, I'm going to start with my agent, Holly Root. Authors are always supposed to have just the right words to say what they want to say, but I'm not sure how to express the gratefulness I have for the way Holly is always there, ready to help and encourage and keep my projects on track. Thank you!

Then there is Dominique Raccah, whose wonderful dream to be a publisher provided me a place at Sourcebooks, where my dream to be an author continues to come true. Thank you, Dominique, for being brave and fearless in finding a way to accomplish truly good things for so many people.

And to Todd Stocke, who undauntingly finds ways to propel Sourcebooks to great heights, thanks for all you do.

To my editor, Steve Geck, a master at knowing just what my manuscript needs: thank you for always pointing the way to a better book.

And what can I say about the entire Sourcebooks team? The words *hardworking* and *fabulous* are two that come to mind, but there are so many more. Every author should be as lucky as me to work with a team like this!

I'm always grateful for my writer pals, those in Florida and those in Illinois. Over many years, Samantha's story has gone through so many revisions that some of you may not even recognize her anymore. But know that I couldn't have gotten this story to where it is today without all of you along the way.

As always, thank you to my mom and dad for all your love and support.

And a ginormous thank-you isn't nearly enough for Ron and Chaylee, because they're the ones who have to live with a writer, which isn't always the easiest thing to do. And to Ginger, who keeps me company in my office.

And most of all, I'm thankful to God for the redemption I get to rest in because of His great love.

ABOUT THE AUTHOR

When Nancy finds herself on a road trip, she's sure to bring along: plenty of car snacks, a couple of small bottles of hand sanitizer (filled to the tippy top), and all her favorite CDs for marathon sing-alongs. Traveling companions find her car snacks satisfying and think the hand sanitizer comes in handy, but those don't make up for the dreadful singing voice Nancy uses to belt out her favorite songs while she heads down the highway.

When Nancy isn't on a road trip, she lives in the Chicago area with her husband and daughter and the cutest five-pound cockapoo anyone has ever seen. When she's not enjoying car snacks on the road and chasing germs with hand sanitizer, she's eating lots of Chicago pizza. Thick crust. Thin crust. She loves it all!

Visit nancyjcavanaugh.com or @nancyjcavanaugh on Twitter to find out more about Nancy and her other books.